THE HEALING POWER OF FAJITAS

THE HEALING POWER OF FAJITAS

a novel

Kathleen Bateman

Copyright 2015 by Kathleen Bateman

Published in the United States by CreateSpace

ISBN 0692496874

ISBN 13: 9780692496879

For the nurses, and for Herb, who always believed

Acknowledgements

Thank you to my Editor, Leslie Ann Engle for the many hours of loving help and encouragement.

Thank you to my graphic artist and daughter, Elissa Bateman Martin, for her invaluable help and talent.

And finally, thank you to my friends and nurses who read rough drafts and were the inspiration for much of this story.

Unlocking the car door, a wave of superheated air enveloped her with a strength-sapping force. She liked to keep the windows rolled down a little in the steamy Houston heat but her husband worried that someone would steal the car. "You always roll them down too much. Just one-half inch is all, Annie. Somebody can get their whole arm in and get the doors unlocked with the amount of space you leave." The downside of following Ben's directions was that the half-inch opening allowed less than one millionth of the hot air to escape from the oven-like atmosphere of the car's interior. But Annie knew the one time that she disobeyed directions would be the one time a band of experienced car thieves would invade the hospital parking lot, on the look-out for an eight year old Toyota with windows gaping open, begging to be stolen. As a result, by the time the air conditioner was blowing cold air, small drops of sweat were tickling Annie's back and her face was flushed a bright pink.

The journey home in progress, she flipped on the radio. Sounds of the sixties, even after these years, caused old memories to float to the surface of her mind: riding around in the car with Ben, singing their certain song together (inwardly smiling at Ben's one-note vocal range), and scenes of one of the few college dances they attended flitted by. He could dance like a professional, in her eyes. Annie, on the other hand, had been brought up in the Church of Christ, where dancing was forbidden. On the few occasions she had sneaked out to a high school dance, it had pretty much been a disaster. She could do no more than slide her feet together, "slow-dance" a little. Her natural lack of rhythm coupled with her guilt at even trying to dance were a guarantee of failure. Ben had always understood her limitations. They just didn't matter to him.

It was so wonderful to be loved. All through high school Annie was the lonely, shy girl who wore glasses. Nowadays, glasses were stylish and some people actually wore glasses with plain lenses in them as a fashion statement. This was truly amazing, bordering on the unbelievable to Annie. The only glasses she fondly remembered were her first ones, cute little red frames she got in the fifth grade. What utter wonder she felt when she looked out of the window at the eye doctor's office and saw the actual leaves on the trees, rather than soft green blobs. The next day she marched into her class wearing her beautiful red glasses, excited to see everything so clearly. Within a few short minutes one of the boys, Bobby Lovacço, was making fun of her, calling her "four eyes." She had no clue what he was talking about until one of her friends told her that he was referring to her glasses. It didn't take long to go from happiness to utter dejection. From then on, she wore her glasses as a necessity, but hated every pair. Her senior year she finally saved up enough babysitting money to buy herself contact lenses. No allotments for beauty in the family budget. "Those are just a vanity we can't afford, my dear," her mother had said in response to her pleas and tears, impassively stirring fruit cocktail into the red Jell-O that in a few hours would become the soft squishy, dessert Annie detested. Annie had always believed that once she shed the ugly glasses, she would be beautiful, no longer afraid, with classmates seeking her out for friendship and acceptance. She walked into class the next day, head held just a little higher, eyes blinking and tearing as the new contacts slid around, the budding sensation of beauty beginning to form in her brain. Bobby Lovacco, still a hovering presence in many of Annie's classes, casually ended her hopes, and walked on with a jaunty whistle, unaware of the destruction he had just caused.

"What's wrong with your eyes? Did you get contacts? You looked better in glasses." It was then Annie realized that she needed more than a set of contact lenses.

Pulling into the driveway she put those memories away, shutting and snapping with a click, the little coin purse in her brain where she kept them. Ben was just pulling into the driveway at the same time. It was good to get home.

MEMORANDUM

STATUS: PRIORITY
SUBJECT: CLOCK-IN PROCEDURE
TO: ALL HOSPITAL PERSONNEL
FROM: ADMINISTRATION
WHEN YOU CLOCK IN FOR DUTY AT YOUR DESIGNATED TIME CLOCK, PLEASE REMEMBER TO OBSERVE PROPER PROCEDURE. DO NOT CLOCK IN MORE THAN 7 MINUTES BEFORE SHIFT IS TO BEGIN. NO EXCEPTIONS! IF YOU CLOCK IN MORE THAN 1 MINUTE AFTER SHIFT IS TO BEGIN, YOU WILL BE COUNTED TARDY. (THREE TARDIES IN 1 MONTH WILL RESULT IN A WRITTEN WARNING – SEE PREVIOUS MEMO ON TARDY GUIDELINES). ALSO, DO NOT CONGREGATE AROUND TIME CLOCK. THIS CAN CAUSE IMPEDEMENT OF TRAFFIC FLOW IN THE HALLWAYS.

After a good night's sleep, which made her absence from the hospital seem but a brief pause, the buzzing angry bee of the alarm clock rudely jarred Annie awake at 5:15. Long ago to increase her sleep time, she had streamlined her morning preparation, and completing it in robot-like fashion, she was en route to the hospital by 5:30.

Sipping her coffee, it was soothing to drive while much of the rest of the city slept. Feelings of the noble call of nursing, being there at inconvenient times to care for patients, edged in on Annie's thoughts as she drove.

Walking in from the parking lot she came upon another co-worker trudging along in the darkness, towards the light of the lobby of the professional building that housed Day Surgery. Mary called out a cheery, "Hi Annie! Boy, it's dark this morning," as if darkness at 5:45 in the morning was an unusual event. "We have a really full schedule today -- twenty-five patients, unless somebody cancels. Five of those are Dr. Ball's patients."

"We'll probably have twenty patients, then," Annie replied matter-of-factly. "Sometimes I wonder if he ever examines his patients before surgery. We had to cancel three last week, all because of high blood pressure, and the patients got really upset. He just never learns. And that Old Spice after-shave – he must shower in it every day."

Just the thought of having to inhale the scent of Dr. Ball's Old Spice this early in the morning made her a little queasy. Mary was still happily talking in this rather one-sided conversation about a recipe she had tried last night from her new favorite cookbook, *Fifty Ways to Cook Ground Meat*. She was one of those people who could wake up and quickly get a flow of words going. Annie was just the opposite. It took awhile for coherent thoughts to form, much less a chatty conversation at 5:45 AM.

A gaggle of nurses surrounded the time clock at 5:57 AM. In direct disobedience of the memo, traffic flow was slightly impeded. There was simply nowhere else to stand. Annie joined the rest of the staff, each clocking in with military efficiency. The repetitive "buzz-click, buzz-click" as the clock's printer scanned and entered the time had its own secret message from the hospital – "you belong to me now . . . buzz-click . . . you belong to me now." It caused a dull heaviness – hearing that sound, a prisoner-like sensation, felt by all, but acknowledged by none.

The patients, of course, didn't know about the clock-in rules and regulations, not having read the memo. Thus, when Annie along with the other nurses walked around to the Day Surgery waiting room, it was full of patients, many of whom looked up as if to say, "There you are . . . finally!"

The phone at the pre-op desk was ringing as Annie rounded the corner.

"Trenton James General Hospital, Day Surgery, Annie speaking, how may I help you?" This was the required statement to be made each and every time one answered the phone, a result of someone in Administration attending a customer-friendly seminar. Because of always being rushed, her greeting usually tumbled out as "TrentnJames genrulospitaldaysugeannis peakinhwmayhelpu,"not the most customer-friendly greeting, in Annie's opinion. When the new rule was announced amidst grumbling and mutters, Annie wanted to stand up in the meeting, and with enthusiastically waving hand add, I know, why don't we include the day, time and the temperature too? Only fear of having that proposal accepted stopped her.

When the new telephone rule began, most of the staff doctors (being in a continually hurried state themselves) tended to simply interrupt the extended telephone greeting mid-syllable with a terse, irritated comment, "It's Dr. Smith, I know I'm talking to Day Surgery, I need scheduling . . ."

This time it was the hospital lab tech, Bill, on the other end of the phone. Since he had to answer the phone the same way, he didn't get irritated.

"One of the specimens y'all sent over yesterday didn't have the nurse's initials on the patient label so we threw it out. You'll have to redraw the specimen if you need the CBC."

No, we don't actually need the report. The doctor ordered it as a little joke. The irritating snap, snap, as Bill jawed his gum, made Annie want to yell in her most teacher-like voice, " Spit that out, and I mean NOW, mister."

That wasn't a very good "team buddy" attitude. "Team buddy" was another weird result of someone in administration attending a seminar on interdepartmental cooperation. "Remember, we're on the same team, buddy" was supposed to remind everyone to work together. It seemed to be about as effective as the telephone-answering rule.

"Sorry about that. What was the name on the lab requisition?" Annie answered. Sigh. The fact that only a set of initials was missing, which could be quickly corrected, seemed beyond the ability of some of the lab techs to comprehend. Charla and Amy were the only two who got it. And as luck would have it, Bill was the lab tech on duty.

There was nothing to be done except redraw the blood and send it to the lab to be run STAT, then just hope and pray that the results were back on the chart before surgery.

The rush was on to get the 7:30 patients ready in a timely manner and there was a whiff of tension in the air. Mixed with the strange aroma that was unique to all hospitals, both patients and nurses felt the edge of sharpness. It was important that the first cases start on schedule, or the rest of the day would be spent playing catch-up.

Although this particular day surgery unit was in a separate building, it was still a part of the hospital and often very ill inpatients from the hospital ended up using one of the operating rooms in the day surgery; one room could hold an ambulatory patient for minor foot surgery, while the next room held a patient from the hospital comatose and with multiple tubes and machines.

Annie picked up a chart of one of the first patients on the schedule and walked out to the waiting room to call out the name. The old man sat along the edge of the room, his face hardened and jaw clinched. He cradled his left arm in his right, as if he were holding a baby. He was small, wiry, and (as is so often the case) accompanied by a round, substantial-looking wife.

"Don't touch that arm!" they both warned Annie sternly, almost in unison. She introduced herself and led them back to the pre-op room to prepare him for his procedure. Mr. Morris was to have an injection into the nerves supplying the hurting arm, in an effort to lessen his pain. He was not an eloquent man and he snapped one word answers to her many necessary nursing assessment questions. His hands gave evidence of his life:

the skin thick and hardened, nicks and little scars scattered over them like thorns on a cactus. The fingernails were so short that callous ridges of skin curled up around them and a blackish bruise darkened his right thumb-nail. These hands depicted the story of a hard-working man who probably endured a lot of bruises without complaining, but who now was almost overcome by his present pain. Although his doctor wasn't sure of the cause, it was believed to be related to a recent case of the shingles.

Annie was touched by his struggle to even be civil in his conversation to her, when he was in such obvious pain. She shortened the questions as much as she could and assured him that as soon as the operative consent was signed, she would call the doctor and ask for pain medicine for him. As she helped him into the hospital gown, his left arm was so exquisitely sensitive he could not even let her slip the gown sleeve on. One shoulder bare, he looked like a small forlorn Tarzan. His wife, who had been guard-ing over him (against Annie, at times it felt), gradually seemed to soften as she saw Annie's concern about the pain.

She voiced a silent prayer as she began to look for a vein in the one "good" arm for the IV needle. This was one vein she didn't want to miss on the first attempt.

"Are you sure you can hit the vein?" he asked, misreading her delibera-tions as a sign of possible incompetence. Of course it was the pain talking, saying, "I can't take much more."

Her prayer was answered and the IV was quickly started. After a merci-fully quick return call from his doctor, she returned with a dose of Fentanyl, knowing it should relieve his pain within minutes.

When she stopped back by to check on Mr. Morris, although the pain wasn't gone, it was better. He spoke a quick, "I can stand it now" as his stretcher was being wheeled back to the operating room for his procedure.

Annie moved on to the next patient. There was always another patient waiting.

As she sat at the pre-op desk a few hours later, she noticed a movement from the corner of her eye. Annie looked up through the glass window that separated pre-op from the progressive recovery area. What had caught her eye was the wave of an arm. It was Mr. Morris, sitting in a wheelchair, being readied for discharge. He motioned to her and she quickly made her way to him. She asked how his pain level was and he replied tersely, "some better." What he did next surprised her though. He reached out, and with his "good" arm gave her a military salute. He looked intently and seriously into her eyes and then said, "I'm honored to have met you." Spoken with such dignity and unexpected grace, those words from this rough-hewn man were all the more touching. This was one of those little gifts that reminded her why she had become a nurse.

As Annie walked back to pre-op her co-worker, Christine, looked up.

"What's wrong? Are you okay? Why are your eyes red?" Christine's gift of observation -- a good nursing skill most days – could be irritating at times. This was one of them.

Annie was pretty sure that Christine was the person that the term "anal retentive" had been developed to describe. She seemed to delight at finding little odds and ends that others had left unfinished or undone. "You didn't date all four sides of the assessment sheet," she would say, quietly holding up the flapping, double-folded paper, indisputable proof for anyone to see. Annie could only look blankly at the incriminating evidence. She was accurate on the big things but not always as concerned about the smaller details, of which there were many. This made a perfect set-up for Christine – having a co-worker whose work she could methodically inspect and find some incomplete detail. Annie would generally tolerate these little rebukes and reminders. But sometimes, on some days, it was just one thing too much. Once, to get even, Annie had inspected one of Christine's charts and found a blank space where she had forgotten to enter her initials. When Christine was shown the minor error, she cried. That pretty much took all the fun out of it for Annie. She realized then it was just too important for Christine to be perfect. And in the end, Annie would have trusted her with her life.

In pre-op once all the patients had been checked in and gone to surgery, the work was far from being done. Occasionally other nurses from the hospital units would come through, glance at the empty pre-op rooms in the afternoon and make comments like, "Boy, I wish I worked here. Y'all have it made!" That pronouncement was completely erroneous and Christine could not resist making an angry defense. "No, we DO NOT have it made. We still have to assess patients for tomorrow, get all the rooms ready, and . . ." At some point, she was usually quietly interrupted by disbelieving snickers as the skeptical nurses ambled back to the hospital where they didn't have it made.

So that afternoon found Annie and Christine at the pre-op desk, surrounded by a small mountain of charts in the process of trying to methodically check each and bring it to completion. What would seem a routine paper-assembling job was complicated by frequent interruptions. The glass partition that separated pre-op and progressive recovery was a key factor. Progressive recovery during the afternoons was usually a bustling place full of patients in various stages of recovery. When a patient went to the bathroom and turned on the blinking call light for help, it added a K-Mart "blue light special" atmosphere. The progressive recovery nurses could look through the glass and see two nurses in pre-op sitting down. Though it was completely reasonable for them to sit to compile charts, this seemed to infuriate some of the progressive recovery nurses. Frequently there would be irritated looks through the glass, but most often it was more than that.

"Could you come wheel this patient to the front for a quick smoke, Annie? He's waiting for his ride and they are running late. He's dying for a cigarette. I just can't leave right now," Lee implored, as she slid the glass window open a notch.

Annie looked through the partition at a patient sitting in the wheelchair directly behind Lee. He was dressed, and he was drumming his fingers on the arm of the wheelchair, crossing and uncrossing his legs, looking on edge. An eye patch taped at a jaunty angle over his left eye gave him a faintly pirate-like appearance. Though Annie wasn't a smoker she had sympathy for them. Her dad had been a life-long smoker who had repeatedly tried to quit. Now that she thought of it, she reflected that she was a pretty good second-hand smoker. As a child growing up, her position in the car was always in the back seat, directly behind her dad, who most days drove with the window down. That effectively funneled ninety percent of his smoke back to his eldest daughter. But he was a good daddy in spite of that small flaw. Annie looked up to see Lee staring at her expectantly.

"I'm sorry. Sure I can run down, if he can make it quick."

The patient, hearing a possible rescuer, hollered out, "Just give me five minutes, lady, I promise!"

"Chris, I'll be right back. That guy is about to jump out of his chair to get a smoke." No response from Christine, who was a militant anti-smoker.

Annie made a quick and quiet exit to progressive recovery and began wheeling the patient down the hallway towards the elevator.

"Little lady, I sure thank you, I know ya'll are busy, but . . ."

"It's okay, but it will have to be a quick smoke, you understand? By the way, I'm Annie."

"Hey, Annie, I'm Walt. I wouldn't have had to bother you if my ride had come on time. I wish I could quit these things. I've tried I don't know how many times." This was said as he pulled the cigarette out of the package. In one easy motion he placed it in his mouth, flicking the lighter lid up and down repeatedly, waiting to finally make it to the outside world.

They were whizzing down the lobby at a good clip when they passed the nursing supervisor, Nita. She nodded and then spoke up.

"Sir, this is a non-smoking facility."

"I'm just wheeling him outside, Mrs. Stromeyer, for a quick smoke. He really needed one," Annie interjected.

Mrs. Stromeyer leaned over and spoke in a loud whisper to Annie, "We are a health care facility, and smoking is not a healthy habit. I'm sure you are aware of that. You are assisting a patient to damage his health, do you realize that?"

Walt had overheard enough. "For crying out loud, I know all about my health. I just needed five minutes and this lady was kind enough to give it to me."

Nita spoke to them both as she walked away. "By all means, don't let me keep you from your task."

Annie felt an uncomfortable silence. She didn't know what to say to Walt but he was so intent on the cigarette, he didn't expect conversation. As Annie stood next to Walt on the shaded sidewalk, the breeze briskly drove his smoke directly into her face and she thought again of her dad fondly. When they got back to the unit and Annie returned to pre-op, Christine wrinkled her nose and said, "Did you smoke too?"

"Sorry, his smoke blew right back on me."

Christine said no more. She merely breathed loudly and shifted papers around noisily. This had its desired effect on Annie – guilt for abandoning Christine. It was a lose/lose situation for Annie, who seemed to attract and hold guilt with a magnetic force.

The other interruption was the phone, which was presently ringing in steady determination. It was a call from the business office secretary, Maya, who worked at the check-in desk.

"There's a patient here, Mrs. Olmos, who just came down from Dr. Grayson's office. She says she's having surgery here in the morning, but her name isn't anywhere on the surgery schedule for tomorrow. Do you know anything about it?"

"Christine, have you heard anything about a patient Olmos, an "add-on" for Dr. Grayson for tomorrow?"

"No. I wonder if she got scheduled late and the scheduling desk didn't call us. They are supposed to do that the first thing, so we know what's going on. I'll call them."

"I'll go out and talk to the patient, Chris, and see if I can find out anything," Annie replied, leaving Christine dialing the phone.

Approaching the patient she began, "Hi, Mrs. Olmos, I'm Annie, one of the nurses . . ."

At this point, Mrs. Olmos interrupted and began talking rapidly, Spanish words interspersed with English.

"Dr. Grayson, he tell me to go to el day surgery and get mi sangre examen. It will only take five minutes. Is muy importante, I'm for operation en la manana."

"Did he give you any papers for us?" Annie asked without much hope. *But wait, that would make too much sense, then we would know what blood work he wanted done, what surgery was scheduled, etc, etc. All those picky little details.*

"He say you have all the papers. I have to leave to pick up mi husband from his job. Can you get my blood now?" She thrust her arm out, as if Annie were always armed and ready to puncture anyone who walked into her vicinity.

"Mrs. Olmos, we don't have any orders from your doctor. I have to talk to him so I know what kind of blood tests he wants. We also need to have you sign consent for your surgery, ask you some questions, and take your blood pressure. It takes about thirty minutes to do all that, not five."

"The doctor, he told me, just come down here and get mi sangre examen. Cinco minutos only. Why you not talk to him already and get these orders you need. I have to leave to pick up mi husband. Why you stand here? Go call the doctor."

Annie, though it was totally illogical, felt rebuked for not knowing what Dr. Grayson wanted done. However, Mrs. Olmos' suggestion (while not very courteous) was the sensible solution. "Just have a seat in the waiting room, while I call your doctor. I'll be right back."

Sighs of irritation followed as the patient walked away mumbling, not very quietly, "Nobody here knows nuthin'. I got to pick up mi husband." Not wanting to hear that refrain again, Annie retreated to the pre-op desk to see if Christine had found anything out yet.

"Scheduling says they JUST got off the phone from Dr. Grayson, he JUST posted the case. I told them we were supposed to be called as soon as an add-on for the next day was scheduled. It makes us look like idiots when the patient shows up and we don't know anything about it. Then the patient just gets mad at us, and we haven't done any thing wrong. It's not fair."

Annie couldn't have agreed more at another of life's little inequities, but they still needed the doctor's orders.

"I'll give the doctor's office a call and see if we can't get orders. They told the patient it would only take her five minutes to get her blood drawn."

"Why do they do that? They know that's not true. Then the patient gets all mad at us again, and it's not our fault," Christine sighed, an irritated sound much the same as their irritated patient.

While Annie called the doctor's office, Christine offered to bring the patient back and get started on the nursing assessment sheet, briskly jumping up to go get Mrs. Olmos.

Annie dialed the phone and was put on hold with soothing music. Strains of Mozart made quite a contrast to undertones she could hear of Mrs. Olmos fussing as Christine explained that it wasn't her fault. Finally, an interruption to Mr. Mozart!

"Yes, this is Betty. What do you need?"

"This is Annie in Day Surgery. We have Mrs. Olmos down here and she says she needs blood drawn for her surgery tomorrow. We don't have any orders. I need to speak to Dr. Grayson."

" I think we faxed you those orders. You should have them. Have you checked your fax machine?" Annie detected a subtle note as the conversation seemed to be going into "blame shifting" mode. There was an underlying tension between the doctor's office staff and the hospital nurses. The ultimate goal was to avoid the wrath of the physician when things went wrong. The office staff had a distinct advantage as they worked side by side with the doctor while "those nurses" in the hospital were an amorphous mass, filled with endless possibilities of little mistakes. Annie knew that some of the offices had staff that were not above changing the facts to deflect blame.

"Dr. Grayson, I faxed all the orders to Day Surgery an hour ago. THOSE NURSES must have lost it."

But Annie couldn't know that for sure. She could only surmise from Betty's tone. "No, I checked the fax before I called you. The patient didn't bring any papers with her. We have nothing on her." With hopes for a quick solution, she tried to calmly re-state the problem: patient, no orders, no way to take care of her.

"He is with a patient right now. I can't interrupt him," Betty replied, as if that settled the matter.

"Do you know how long it will be before I can talk to him and get some orders on this patient? She can't stay very long." Annie almost found herself adding "she has to pick up her husband."

"No. I'll ask him to call Day Surgery as soon as I see him."

Meanwhile, Mrs. Olmos was growing more irritated at the one hundred questions that Christine was asking in a determined effort to complete the nursing assessment sheet – and leave no blank spaces. The patient was lapsing more and more into Spanish and the whole process was deteriorating. The volume of their voices was increasing in true inverse proportion to the decrease in the level of communication. Why did people think yelling in a different language made it more understandable to the yellee?

"ES IMPOSSIBLE…USTED NO COMPRENDE."

"I AM JUST TRYING TO HELP YOU. IT IS NOT MY FAULT YOUR DOCTOR DIDN'T SEND ANY ORDERS."

Mrs. Olmos wasn't buying it. Annie went to the pre-op room and Mrs. Olmos looked up, a grimace of irritation on her face.

"There you are. This lady asked me too many questions, she no get mi sangre, and I got to go pick up mi esposo. What the doctor tell you?" Mrs. Olmos was getting to the end of her tolerance with Christine and turned her full attention to Annie.

"Mrs. Olmos, I wasn't able to talk to the doctor. He is supposed to call me back with your orders. I'm sorry you have to wait, but we don't know what he wants until we talk to him."

In a quiet sidebar to Christine, they tried to salvage the situation. Christine had found out that the patient took high blood pressure medication so they were safe in drawing a potassium level.

"Does she have diabetes?" Annie asked, wondering about getting a blood sugar level too.

"She said not, but who knows. She's not really listening to my questions. She keeps interrupting me."

" Why don't we get two tubes just to have an extra tube, so she only gets one stick?" Annie didn't have a problem with drawing blood with no orders yet, but her partner did.

"We are not supposed to draw blood with no orders."

"Well, yes, technically that's true, but I don't think it's going to hurt anything to get one or two extra tubes, Christine."

Christine was just opening her mouth to give her defense. A change of tactics was needed.

"Maybe I'll just try Dr. Grayson one more time. It's almost 5:00, the office will be closing."

Sure enough, when Annie redialed the doctor's office at 4:55, it had already been switched over to the answering service.

"Dr. Grayson is no longer in the office. Dr. Alfonse is taking calls. Do you want me to page him for you?" the paging operator stated in a flat nasal tone.

"Dr. Alfonse doesn't know this patient so that won't help. I need to talk to Dr. Grayson," Annie responded tersely, hearing Mrs. Olmos in the background, stating her oft-spoken announcement, "I got to pick up mi esposo at work.'"

"I'm sorry, Dr. Grayson is not taking calls. Will there be anything else?"

Sigh.

Outwardly gracious in the face of total defeat, Annie answered in her best team buddy voice, "No, thanks anyway, we'll work something out."

"Mrs. Olmos, I'm sorry the doctor's office is closed and we . . ."

"You peoples, why you no call him when I tell you to? I got to . . ."

"Yes, I know, pick up your husband," Annie knew the drill by now. Part of her wanted to say, "Just go then, but don't plan on being ready for surgery." The other part of her felt sorry for this lady who didn't understand any of this procedure and hadn't been told what to expect.

"What surgery is the doctor doing, Mrs. Olmos?"

"I not a doctor, no se how the doctor do surgery," Mrs. Olmos replied, irritated at one more ridiculous question.

Deep breath. "Mrs. Olmos, why did you go to the doctor?"

"Oh, this little spot on my neck, it got blood on my good dress." Mrs. Olmos reached back and pushed the collar of her blouse down. Christine and Annie both looked at the black, irregular, ominous looking area that was suddenly revealed. Their eyes met across Mrs. Olmos' back and they shared a solemn moment, simultaneously silently diagnosing the malignant melanoma, realizing what their patient did not. This was a life-threatening "spot." Inwardly, they both softened towards this feisty, irritating patient.

Christine carefully instructed the patient not to eat or drink after midnight and to get to Day Surgery promptly at 6:00 AM in the morning. They could get one of the anesthesia team to assess and write some orders on the patient or maybe get Dr. Grayson early, so the patient could be ready to go to surgery at 7:30 AM promptly. It would be hectic, but with a lot of luck and no complications, it was just possible.

Mrs. Olmos left in the same way she came – irritated and still muttering in her Spanglish that needed no translation.

Annie and Christine both returned to the pre-op desk, still covered with partially assembled charts to be completed before they could leave. In the midst of putting a chart together, Christine suddenly commented, "Oh, great, not him."

Annie waited for the explanation, but after a few moments, when none was forthcoming, she gave up and asked.

"What did you mean, not him?"

"What are you talking about?"

Annie hated these weird little non-conversations that seemed to develop when she was tired or Christine was tired. Right now they were both tired.

"You said, a minute ago, 'oh, great, not him.' Not who?"

Christine looked intently at Annie and for a moment Annie thought she was going to deny the whole thing. But something finally clicked.

"Oh, yeah, I meant – remember that smelly old man that was here a few months ago, Mr. Allen? Well, he's on the schedule tomorrow. He cusses all the time and won't cooperate. Would you take him this time?"

"Chris, I don't even remember him. He must have been here on my day off or something. Sure, I'll take him." *He can't be all that bad.*

"Oh, yes, and that patient Mrs. Nguyen, she's seventy-five. I bet she doesn't speak English. You ought to save room one for her where the language phone is."

"Chris, you don't know, she may speak English fluently. You shouldn't judge people like that just because of a name."

"I'm not judging, Annie. I'm using common sense, for Pete's sake."

Realizing they were both tired and Annie's little condescending lectures weren't going to change anything, she decided to just shut up and work.

Anita from Housekeeping came softly through the unit, wet-mopping and dusting. She nodded, and gave the nurses a little inter-hospital news as she worked.

"JCAHO is coming through in two months, I hear."

Inward groans from Annie, as she mused how complicated life was with the addition of JCAHO.

JCAHO, short for Joint Commission on Accreditation of Healthcare Organizations, was the inspection agency for any hospital that wanted to get paid for Medicare services. Every two years the JCAHO inspectors came, peering around corners and asking questions. Although the propaganda message from hospital administration was, "We don't have anything to fear from Joint Commission. They are just here to keep the quality of care high and that's what we all want," everyone on the nursing staff knew better. From top management down, everyone gradually became petrified with a tangible fear that seemed to seep through the air conditioning vents, pervading the entire hospital. For several months before the inspection, management began a gradual descent to what Annie called "inspection madness". The nursing managers went to a slowly escalating number of meetings, from which they returned increasingly harried and tense.

Annie remembered Janet, her nursing manager, storming back after one meeting, going to the sink in pre-op, jerking the door to the cabinet underneath open and spying some bottles of disinfectant sitting where they always sat.

"This is NOT allowed. Get these things out of here. There is to be nothing in this cabinet," she ordered, as if she had discovered body parts hidden there.

Annie couldn't resist asking, "What is the point of having a cabinet if we can't store anything there?"

Normally Janet would have smiled and made some comment at the absurdity of some of these rules, but she was already, unbeknownst to Annie, infected with "inspection madness."

"I really don't need any smart comments, Annie. Just get rid of the damn bottles."

The under-sink cabinet episode culminated in the installation of locks, which insured that the cabinets remained completely empty and unusable.

Finally, at 6:20 PM, the last chart was put together, labeled with time tape and put into the chart slot. It had been a long time since arising at 5:15 AM, and Annie and Christine were more than ready to head for home. The quietness of the empty Day Surgery unit was broken by the ring of the phone. Tempting as it was not to answer, Annie couldn't resist picking up the receiver.

"Daysurganniespkhowcanihlpu," Spoken in a flat-tire monotone, the greeting was made devoid of meaning.

"Who am I speaking to?" The crisp tone of the voice had an edge and the conversation had not even begun.

"Sorry, I said that pretty fast. This is Annie, one of the nurses in Day Surgery. Can I help you?"

"Well, I just wonder if you don't need to take the refresher in-service on telephone etiquette, Anna. I couldn't understand a word you said." While Annie was mulling over a response, the voice continued.

"I am trying to reach your manager, Janet, to notify her of a meeting tomorrow. Her phone line must have rolled over to yours. Would you take a message for me to her?"

" Sure, I'd be glad to. Who is the message from?"

"Well, really Anna, it is obviously from me. What kind of question is that?"

"Ma'am, you never have told me who you are," Annie responded, trying to sound calm, resisting her urge to shout into the phone, "I think I know someone who has forgotten her telephone etiquette."

"Of course I told you when you answered. But one more time, this is Nita Stromeyer. Do I need to spell that?"

"Uh, no, I've got it. What is the message?"

"All unit managers need to be in the executive dining room at 8:00 AM sharp for a budget meeting. Got that?"

" Yes Nita, I will put it on her desk so she will see it as soon as she comes in, OK?"

"That will be fine, Anna. One other thing, you know the hospital is having a budget crunch and all overtime must be approved by unit managers. Since you are still here after hours, I assume you have gotten this approved by Janet."

"Well, no, Janet has already left. Her phone line rolled to me."

Remember, that's how I ended up talking to you.

"So, Anna, you are here without approval from your manager then. This is not good, not good at all."

" Nita, I would much rather be at home. Christine and I were getting tomorrow's charts ready. It's not something we can just walk off and leave."

" You mean there is someone else working overtime? What other things are going on over there that have not been approved? You know I've been noting how many times I come on a unit and nurses are chattering away on the telephone instead of getting their work done. I wonder if this may not be part of your problem here, Anna. Too much telephone time."

I couldn't agree with you more, Nita.

"Yes, well, Nita, we have to answer the phone when it rings and that happens a good bit during the day." Annie began doodling on the note pad in front of her and then noticed it was a sword with blood dripping down to the bottom of the page. Christine had given up all pretence of finishing closing doors and turning off lights and was sitting listening.

"Yes, of course you have to answer the phone, Anna. Don't be ridiculous. It's just something I'm pointing out to you to be aware of."

"Thank you, Nita. I appreciate your pointers. Was there anything else?"

"No, Anna, you and Christine need to scoot and clock out as quickly as you can. Be sure you get an approval from Janet in the morning. And next time, try to organize your time better so you don't have to work late. Okay, then . . ." Click.

"So much for telephone etiquette. She just hung up, didn't say goodbye or anything. She is so irritating."

Christine, recognizing a kindred spirit in Nita, was suddenly overcome with compassion and understanding.

"Annie, I think Nita was just tired. She is very conscientious and wants the rules followed, that's all."

2

MEMORANDUM

STATUS: PRIORITY
SUBJECT: LANGUAGE PHONE
TO: ALL NURSING PERSONNEL
FROM: RISK MANAGEMENT
THE LANGUAGE PHONE IS THE ONLY LEGALLY ACCEPTABLE METHOD OF COMMUNICATING WITH A NON ENGLISH-SPEAKING PATIENT. DO NOT USE ANOTHER HOSPITAL EMPLOYEE WHO SPEAKS THE PATIENT'S LANGUAGE. THIS COULD BE MEDICALLY/LEGALLY UNSAFE. LANGUAGE PHONE USAGE REQUIRES A 10 DIGIT ENTRY CODE. EACH STAFF IS RESPONSIBLE FOR OBTAINING HIS/HER CODE # FROM YOUR UNIT MANAGER. LET'S ALL WORK TOGETHER TO ELIMINATE ANY RISK OF COMMUNICATING ILLEGALLY!

"I hope Mrs. Olmos is here so we can have her ready on time." These were the first words Christine spoke to Annie as they met at the time clock. "I repeated several times to get here right at 6:00 AM and how important it was, but she was still going on about how we don't know what we are doing and picking up her husband."

"Well, here's hoping your good instructions got through," Annie replied as they headed towards the check-in desk.

Annie scanned the patient registration sheet and Mrs. Olmos' name wasn't on it, which really irritated Christine, though Annie wasn't surprised.

"Well, we'll get blamed again when she isn't ready and it isn't our fault." Blame-avoidance was one of Christine's core values. They agreed to do a "double-team" on this particular patient when she did decide to arrive. Christine and Annie each picked up a chart for the other 7:30 cases and began the check-in process.

Mrs. Nguyen was a tiny Vietnamese lady, barely five feet tall. She was dressed in a long, simple garment, the same type she had worn all her life in Vietnam; coming to a completely different country and culture, many things had changed, but not her wardrobe. Her hair was pulled back tightly in a bun, making her look even smaller. She had a gracious manner and sweet smile, nodding to Annie repeatedly as she followed her back to the pre-op check-in room. She was accompanied by her daughter who nodded and smiled just like her mother. When Annie asked the daughter if she spoke English, she only nodded affirmatively. This was not a very encouraging sign of the extent of the daughter's English, but Annie hoped maybe she was just shy.

"Mrs. Nguyen, have you had anything to eat or drink since midnight?" There was an extended conversation in Vietnamese between the two ladies, and then a unified nodding of heads. Annie once again asked the daughter, "Are you sure you understand English okay?"

"I understand some, not too much," the daughter finally confessed and what would have been a routine fifteen to twenty minute check-in procedure suddenly shifted to a much more labor-intensive process. No one on the nursing staff in Day Surgery spoke Vietnamese so Annie excused herself and went to the Language telephone located in pre-op room one, remembering Christine's opinion she had so blatantly ignored. Sure enough, there was another patient in pre-op one, which necessitated a hasty relocation of all parties. When she got a Vietnamese interpreter on the line the patient, her daughter, and Annie huddled around the speaker-phone like Dorothy, the Tin Man, and the Cowardly Lion meeting the Wizard of Oz. Slowly but surely, the many questions were answered. Ominous and scary phrases saturated the wording on the consent, "risk of death" being the most obvious. There were six different places to be initialed. Mrs. Nguyen seemed exhausted by the time the consent had been translated.

At 6:25 AM Christine stuck her head in the door. "Mrs. Olmos is finally here. Can you help me?"

No way Christine could get that patient ready without some help. Mrs. Nguyen was getting changed into a hospital gown as Annie left the room.

Mrs. Olmos was accompanied by her hardworking husband, all three daughters, and an assortment of grandchildren clumped together in a tight group. Annie admired the way many in the Hispanic culture responded to illness as an "all-for-one and one-for-all" commitment. It gave the waiting room a family reunion feeling, though it was noisy at times.

"Only two people can come back to the pre-op room," Christine made the announcement in the general direction of the Olmos clan. This edict was promptly ignored and they all rose in unison as the patient stood up. Finally Mrs. Olmos, her husband, and one daughter came back with Annie and Christine. A few minutes later, the second daughter came back followed eventually by daughter number three. That meant the grandchildren had an unexpected gift of freedom resulting in yelps, laughter and the sound of little running feet could be heard echoing down the hallway at times.

Christine asked the check-in questions as Annie took the vital signs, applied the name bracelet and readied the hospital gown. Of course, there were still no orders on the chart, so it was impossible to complete everything. One of the anesthesiologists, Dr. Dade, was there early, having been alerted by Christine and came in to assess Mrs. Olmos. He ordered an EKG. Annie brought the EKG machine to the already crowded pre-op room. When the EKG machine came into the room, bodies pressed together side by side, but there simply was no room. With two of the daughters and Mr. Olmos briefly out, Annie and Christine attached the leads and within five minutes had a printout of the EKG. The results from the potassium level were normal, and shortly Dr. Grayson walked in with a curt, "Well, are we ready to go?"

"We need to get the operative permit signed, sir, and . . ." Christine began.

"Well, get it signed and let's get going, I have a busy schedule. Y'all are supposed to have things ready to go by 7:15." He gave an impatient look to Mrs. Olmos and family as if to say, "See, I'm ready to go. These nurses aren't." Mrs. Olmos and company nodded heads in silent assent.

Thanks a lot folks, for your support. Score: Doctor Grayson one, Nurses zero.

"We need Doctor's written orders, sir, for the correct wording on the permit," Christine's flat rejoinder, words like lead pellets falling heavily.

"Wide local excision of mole on the back, it's written on the surgery schedule," Dr. Grayson answered back abruptly.

"Yes sir, but we are supposed to follow hospital procedure which states . . ."

Dr. Grayson was not in the mood for an explanation of the correct procedure. "If you nurses would use a little common sense, we could get things started on time around here."

Hoping to veer Christine off her present course, which was usually a futile effort, Annie quickly brought in the consent and began a rush job of getting Mrs. Olmos to sign it. His stiffly starched lab coat rustled as Dr. Grayson turned and said, "I'm going back to change into my scrubs. See you in a few minutes, Mrs. Olmos. Have her brought back to the OR."

Christine's silence was ominous. Fortunately, the anesthesiologist, Dr. Dade came in and began wheeling Mrs. Olmos to the OR which diffused things considerably. However, Mrs. Olmos, in parting, managed to toss a small but effective verbal grenade.

"I knew you peoples not know what you doing, yesterday you no call the doctor when I tell you."

Suddenly, the fast-moving procession came to a halt. Mrs. Olmos had called out a command in tones that brooked no disobedience.

"Stop now."

Dr. Dade pulled to a stop and the stretcher carrying Mrs. Olmos stood motionless in the doorway to the OR, causing a repeated click of the electric eye on the automatic door-opener sensor.

"My rosary. I got to have my rosary with me."

For the first time since meeting this patient, there was a scared edge in her voice. Mr. Olmos had already started scratching around in his pockets in a hurried search for the needed object. But Christine, still smarting from the unwarranted rebuke from Dr. Grayson, stepped in. "No ma'am, that is not allowed. You can't take anything back with you. It could get lost in the linen, or somewhere in the operating room and then you would be really upset."

"I got to have my rosary," said as a statement of fact, not a request.

Just then, Mr. Olmos pulled the disputed rosary from his pocket, holding it up like a prize he had just been awarded unexpectedly.

Annie couldn't keep out of this one.

Carefully avoiding eye contact with Christine, she said softly, " Chris, I think we can bend the rules a little this time. I will be responsible for it, okay?" This was all said as she placed the rosary in Mrs. Olmos' outstretched hands.

Dr. Dade began rolling the stretcher forward again and the conversation halted. But Annie knew the conversation was not over. Christine walked back to the desk, shuffled some papers loudly and finally said, "You know that's against the rules, Annie. What if it gets lost?"

"I know, but she sounded like she really did need it. I was just trying to keep her from getting upset."

"And if it gets lost, she won't be upset?"

Annie had no answer for that one, but Teresa provided the needed interruption.

"Hey, you guys, the IV in room one isn't started yet. Should I go do that now, or is there something else more important?"

Thanking Teresa, Annie joined her in Mrs. Nguyen's room to speed up the final preparations. Mrs. Nguyen's doctor, Dr. Nagel, was notorious for being late, and today that was a good thing. Just maybe they would have Mrs. Nguyen ready on time.

Mrs. Nguyen was scheduled for a bronchoscopy to look into her lungs and see what the reason could be for her persistent cough and spitting up blood. She looked very frail and her color concerned Annie and Teresa. Taking her vital signs, Annie placed the oximeter clip on her finger and saw that her oxygen saturation was only 85% – way below the normal of 96 to 100. Mrs. Nguyen didn't like that little clip on her finger put there by this nurse she couldn't understand and kept fiddling with it, causing it to lose contact and the reading to drop to 50 or so which then made the alarm sound, which scared Mrs. Nguyen and made her even more fidgety. It was tempting to turn the alarm off but with an oxygen level already so low, Annie resisted. So the already bustling pre-op area had a whining ding-ding-ding of the oximeter alarm accompanying the many other sounds.

Through the daughter, Annie asked, "Do you use any oxygen at home?"

A shy smile.

Oh well, there would just have to be some blank spaces in this chart. One positive note; finding the blanks would brighten Christine's day. Teresa had the IV started and taped in place before Mrs. Nguyen even realized what had happened. As if on cue, Dr. Nagel walked in. The appearance to him was one of complete efficiency and he mistakenly assumed all were waiting impatiently for his arrival.

"Sorry I was running a little behind," he mumbled under his breath.

"Good morning, sir, we're always glad to see you, even if it is a few minutes late." Teresa reached out and patted Dr. Nagel on the arm in greeting.

"It's always good to see you too, Teresa," Dr. Nagel smiled back.

Annie stood mute, feeling ignored, possibly because she was.

"No problem, sir, I'll let the OR know you are here and ready," Teresa replied, smiling graciously. Teresa's schmooze factor- a number 10. Annie could manage between a 3 or a 4 on good days. Poor Christine was usually hovering at a zero and on bad days slipped into minus territory. It was effortless and natural to Teresa, which made it even more irritating to low schmooze factor people like Christine.

"Oh yes, one more thing, this is not a 'rule-out-TB' case is it? The OR wanted me to ask you." Annie knew this question was a waste of time but had to ask.

"No, of course not, she's negative. What a question!"

This was not a question the nurse would usually ask a doctor, but Dr. Nagel had a quirky habit of posting contagious cases and ignoring special infection control protocol. Annie remembered asking him this same question last month about a sickly looking patient. With Dr. Nagel's denial, her impulse was to shout "liar, liar, pants on fire." Sure enough, the lab results later revealed active TB. Other patients and nurses had needlessly been exposed. To top it off, when Dr. Nagel was notified, he feigned complete surprise. This was really hard to believe since he was a lung specialist and had seen TB many times. Annie hoped that this was not one of those cases because as Teresa was leaning over the patient starting her IV, Mrs. Nguyen had had a sudden coughing spell directly in Teresa's face. Teresa seemed unfazed, but Annie knew that it had scared her. As for Annie, when Mrs. Nguyen was being wheeled back to surgery, she reached out to Annie and hugged her. So there had been plenty of close contact with a possibly contagious little lady.

Annie and Teresa both met at the sink for hand washing. Teresa's hands and arms were covered in soap suds, as she vigorously scrubbed away.

"I think I'm going down to the health nurse and get a chest x-ray. I don't want to get TB. What if I start coughing up blood? Then it's too late."

At that moment Teresa developed a coughing spell and Annie smiled quietly to herself.

"Teresa, I think it's too early to get a chest x-ray just yet." If a nurse worried about every bug she was exposed to, the resultant anxiety could be paralyzing. As a rule, denial worked well for Annie.

Teresa, Christine and Annie finished checking in all the morning surgeries and were ready to start lunch rotations. Teresa announced that she was starving and, using her million-dollar smile, was the first for lunch.

There were just two more cases scheduled at 1:00, but the progressive recovery room was full. This was the last stop before the patient was discharged. Some patients were ready to go twenty minutes after arriving to progressive recovery while others took hours. There were six progressive recovery recliner chairs, upholstered in a vinyl aptly called "puke-green" by the nurses, chosen by an interior decorator who apparently had never worked in a hospital setting. Those ugly chairs could get full and stay full a long time and most days did just that, like a bottleneck on a freeway.

Annie looked through the glass partition window that separated pre-op and progressive recovery. She saw Mrs. Olmos surrounded by her family who were giving her sips of some liquid and chatting and laughing. She waved her hand weakly in Annie's direction. Annie put her papers down and walked to the patient's side.

She probably wants to thank me for letting her take the rosary back to surgery with her, Annie thought. Sometimes, it does pay to bend the rules some.

"Mrs. Olmos, you are all through with your surgery. How do you feel?"

"It no taste good. Bring me something else."

Well really, how irritating can you get! "What would you like?"

"This Coke tastes bad. Bring a new one in a can." Annie complied in silence and quickly excused herself to return to pre-op, glad she didn't have to deal with such an ungrateful patient anymore.

The ringing phone was timely.

"Annie, I am trying to update everyone's record and you don't have any proof of having attended the safety in-service last month." Janet, the Day Surgery Nurse Manager was spending yet another day reviewing everyone's records.

Annie reminded her, "Remember, I was at the in-service and before it was finished you called and asked me to come back to Day Surgery because things were backing up. I never got to take the exit test."

None of these details seemed important to Janet now.

"Annie, you know the safety in-services are mandatory. I expect you to make up what you miss. Everyone has to have a passing exit test in their file."

Annie mumbled an "I'm sorry" and agreed to take the online test that day to get the needed proof in her file.

Janet responded with a comment about how important it was for us all to take personal responsibility. Annie thought that's what she had been doing when she left the meeting early to cover Day Surgery but wisely refrained from comment, as this wasn't the first time her files were not up-to-date.

"Chris, that was Janet. I need to get online and take the safety in-service test."

"Okay, except, did you know Lee never did get to lunch and one of us should relieve her? I'm trying to track down some missing labs for a patient that's having surgery tomorrow, could you do it? I thought you told me you asked if everyone had their break."

Annie didn't answer, realizing she had forgotten Lee. Now it was 2:00 PM, pretty late in the day for someone who had been working since 7:00 AM. She headed back to the progressive recovery and found Lee at Mrs. Nguyen's side, in a vain attempt to go over instructions with the daughter.

"Lee, I'm sorry, I didn't know you hadn't eaten lunch . . ."

Lee quickly interrupted with, "It would help if you asked."

"Let me take over for you. Oh, I think we need to use the language phone with Mrs. Nguyen and her daughter. It'll work better that way." Lee allowed that it was so good to have an expert take over and walked away.

After another 20-minute session on the language phone going over discharge instructions in Vietnamese, Mrs. Nguyen was ready for discharge except her color still looked really crummy to Annie.

"We'll just check her oximeter reading one more time," she spoke to the daughter, who looked puzzled at what this nurse was doing now to her mother.

Mrs. Nguyen meekly extended her finger, finally over her earlier fear of the oximeter. Annie was shocked to see the reading at 76%. There was no way she could discharge Mrs. Nguyen. Annie took her back to the recliner, started oxygen, and put a call into Dr. Nagel. By this time Lee was back from her lunch break.

"What in the world is going on?"

Annie explained that she didn't like the patient's skin color and what her oxygen level was.

"Good grief, Annie, why did you put the oximeter on? You knew her O2 would be low," Lee interjected.

That question was so dumb she couldn't think of an answer. Meanwhile, the ringing phone signaled Dr. Nagel on the line.

"Could you come down and check her? I don't feel comfortable sending her home with her O2 so low."

Dr. Nagel answered that he was not really interested in coming down, as he was in his office and had a waiting room full of patients.

"Just have respiratory therapy give her an Albuterol breathing treatment and then send her home."

"She isn't wheezy, sir. I listened to her lung sounds, they sound kind of faint on the right . . ."

"Just follow my orders, please, Annie. She'll be fine."

"Well, at least he ordered a respiratory treatment, even though he doesn't want to come and see her. I guess I'll get the treatment and then see how she is. I'm not going to send her home if she's not better." Annie spoke these words to no one in particular; mainly to reassure her own mind of what her plan was. In the very back of her mind a possible doctor/nurse conflict loomed, a small dark cloud in the faraway edge of the blue sky.

"Annie, you are not the doctor. He's the responsible one, plus the fact that at our last staff meeting we were told we were keeping patients in progressive recovery too long. We are way over budget," Lee argued.

"Yeah, but shouldn't he at least come and look at her?"

"You know him, he's not going to do that."

Annie knew that was true. But after the breathing treatment, Mrs. Nguyen didn't look that much pinker and was spitting up some blood. Of course, she was doing that before the procedure, but Annie thought it was a little worse. By this time, she wasn't sure she was being objective anymore, so she called Christine.

The two nurses stood side by side assessing the deteriorating situation.

"What's her oxygen level now?" Christine asked. It was up to 84%, which was still horrible.

"You have to call Dr. Nagel back and tell him, Annie."

Dr. Nagel was less than thrilled to be interrupted in his office again and was not impressed at all with the oxygen level.

"She has a problem with her lungs, that's why she came to a lung specialist. Take the oximeter off and send her home. Don't call me again."

What is the deal with taking the oximeter off? Dr. Nagel and Lee must use the same treatment plan, Annie mused.

Once again in her nursing career, Annie felt trapped in the dreaded "Cage of No-Win Decisions." Annie paused for a moment and considered a possible scenario.

Lawyer for the prosecution: "Annie Brown, as a registered nurse, do you or do you not know the normal oxygen saturation levels?"

Annie: "Yes, but this patient came in with low levels on admission."

Lawyer for the prosecution: "But you know as a registered nurse that 84% oxygen saturation is unsafe, do you not?"

Annie: "Yes, but I called the doctor and told him."

Lawyer for the prosecution: "Please answer the question yes or no. A reasonable and prudent nurse would not discharge a patient with an oxygen saturation of 84%, would they?"

Annie: "No, but . . ."

Judge (Interrupting loudly and glaring down at Annie): "I've heard enough. Guilty. Mrs. Brown, you behaved like a mindless robot. Turn in your nursing license before stepping down. You are a disgrace to your profession."

She considered calling the hospital Chief of Staff, but quickly ruled that out. About the only time she could do something that drastic was if blood was spurting from a post operative incision like a fountain, and the surgeon had refused to come.

One other option was to call the anesthesiologist who had been on Mrs. Nguyen's case. Annie checked the chart and saw Dr. March's name. Now, if she were still in the hospital and could come check the patient, maybe things could get fixed.

Dr. March answered Annie's page within a minute. "I'm in the main operating room just finishing a case. I will be over in fifteen minutes. Get a stat chest x-ray and arterial blood gases. Turn up the oxygen and use a face mask if she is a mouth breather, we need to get that saturation up."

Breathing a sigh of relief, Annie and Lee began getting those tasks done. Annie remembered Mr. Than, a Vietnamese employee that worked the evening shift in Central Supply. Although they were supposed to use the language phone, it was just too time-consuming in a situation like this and Mr. Than was always so nice. He was on duty and came right over. He explained about the portable x-ray machine and the blood work and Mrs. Nguyen and her daughter seemed calmer. Her oxygen saturation level was only up to 88% though, still pretty low.

Enter Dr. March. Annie could see that she was concerned, too.

"Where is Dr. Nagel?"

"He says he is not coming down, for me to send her home," Annie answered.

Dr. March made no comment, but shook her head in the smallest wag of disapproval, before asking for the chest x-ray results.

The radiologist came on the line shortly with the terse report, "Your patient has a 40% pneumothorax on the right."

Realizing that this partial collapse of the lung if left untreated could progress to a life-threatening situation, Dr. March went into action. She called Dr. Nagel. He responded in a much more tolerant manner when being called by another doctor. In a very diplomatic manner, she mentioned that in doing her postoperative check on the day surgery patients she noticed Mrs. Nguyen in some distress and ordered a chest x-ray. Annie didn't mind being left out at all. She just wanted Mrs. Nguyen to get treated. Mrs. Nguyen needed to have a chest tube inserted into the right side that would relieve the pressure so the lung could re-expand. Dr. Nagel didn't do this procedure but Dr. Alfonse, a surgeon, just happened to be available, according to Dr. March.

"Would you like for me to speak to Dr. Alfonse and see if he can put the chest tube in right away, Dr. Nagel? You can take care of writing the admission orders and we'll put her in ICU overnight just to keep an eye on her." Dr. March was so smooth in getting this obstinate doctor to say yes, it was almost fun to watch her in action.

Dr. Alfonse called back almost immediately and said he could be there shortly. Annie and Lee had moved Mrs. Nguyen back to the level one recovery room on a stretcher.

"Sandy, can you help us out? We've got to set up for a chest tube insertion now."

Without a word Sandy, the recovery room nurse, began clearing a cubicle, moving a tray stand, and setting up suction equipment. They located the chest tube insertion tray but there was no chest tube. Lee sprinted over the walkway to the hospital Central Supply department to get one and pick up Mr. Than again, who had gone back to his assigned duties. This was no time for the language-line phone. Lee came back with Mr. Than to translate and the permit was being signed just as Dr. Alfonse walked into the recovery room. The procedure itself was very quick. Dr. Alfonse was an experienced surgeon and within minutes, the small tube was easily inserted and in place. In less than a minute, Mrs. Nguyen looked better. Her color pinked up and her saturation was shortly at 90%. For her, that was fantastic. Just when everything was finished, Dr. Nagel strolled into the recovery room. He greeted Dr. Alfonse, thanked him, and patted Mrs. Nguyen on the hand, the picture of a concerned doctor.

"Get an ICU bed, get me an order sheet." This was spoken with a dismissive wave of the hand towards Annie.

"They are holding a bed for us, sir," was Annie's only response. She thought of the day far away when she would make all things right. She had decided a good while back that on her retirement day she would tell all the jerks exactly what she thought of them. Dr. Nagel's position had just moved up a notch on the list.

Within twenty minutes, Annie and Lee were wheeling Mrs. Nguyen on her stretcher down the hospital corridors. The ICU nurses helped move her to a bed, get the monitors and oxygen attached, and get a verbal report from Annie all at the same time. As Annie was preparing to leave one of the nurses said, "What's the deal with all these pneumothoraxes lately? I just had one of this doctor's patients here last week – same thing right after a bronchoscopy."

"Really . . . that does seem kind of unusual, doesn't it?" Annie agreed.

The ICU nurse rolled her eyes. "It makes you wonder about the technique, you know?"

Just then Mrs. Nguyen reached out and grabbed Annie's hand. It was a hand tiny enough to be a child's, yet she held on with surprising strength. ICU was a noisy, scary place, made even more so because Mrs. Nguyen couldn't speak English. She reminded Annie of a small, delicate rabbit captured in the cage-like bars of the side rails that surrounded her. So Annie held on to the soft little rabbit paw for several moments. Then she smiled down at Mrs. Nguyen.

"You're going to be okay now, Mrs. Nguyen." Those reassuring words didn't seem to need translation, as the patient leaned her head back and released her tight grip.

It was 4:30 PM by the time Annie headed back to Day surgery pushing the empty stretcher. Although Mrs. Nguyen was not technically her patient, by the time Annie had intervened and starting calling doctors, Mrs. Nguyen became hers by default. No one else wanted to get involved in the mess. This was fine, except that Annie was assigned to pre-op and there were piles of charts to get ready for tomorrow. If Christine hadn't gotten some help, that pile was probably still sitting and waiting. It wasn't that people weren't willing to help out, but patients outweighed paperwork. It could leave pre-op in somewhat of a mess, though.

Sure enough, pre-op was in somewhat of a mess.

Nita and Janet, along with several of the staff, were in a small huddle to the side of the pre-op desk as Annie rounded the corner.

"Oh, there you are Anna. We are having a brief staff meeting here. Could you join us please?" Nita stood armed with her clipboard in raised defensive position.

She began with a report on how overcrowded the progressive recovery area was. She carefully explained that six chairs were just not enough for the numbers of patients.

Like we all don't know about how overcrowded things are. Please.

Finally she got to the point. "We are opening an overflow unit on the second floor of the hospital where the sleep lab used to be. Tomorrow morning at 6:15 we will all meet over there and I will fill everyone in on the details. Just wanted you to all have a heads-up."

This seemed rather unusual. Nita wasn't known for giving heads-up information to staff. She ended the meeting with a cheery salute of her clipboard and was off. People wandered away in a general air of puzzlement tinged with suspicion.

Annie and Christine were left to plod their way through the mound of charts, getting ready for the next day. It was 6:45 PM by the time the two had finally completed everything. Once again, though, the telephone rang just as they had turned the lights off.

"Should I get it or not?"

"Annie, we are closed. Whatever it is can wait till tomorrow. I've got to get home and get supper started. Enos hates it when I'm this late."

But the ringing seemed so determined and Annie felt powerless to resist it's pleading. Of course, just as she picked the phone up, she became instantly regretful.

What if it was Nita? She would be caught working overtime again. But it was not Nita, thank goodness, although she wasn't overjoyed at the caller's identity.

"This the nurse? This the surgery place where I was?"

"Hello. Yes, this is Day Surgery and this is Annie – one of the nurses. Can I help you?"

"You got to help me. I got home and I no got my rosary. You find it, okay? I hold on?"

"Mrs. Olmos, is that you?"

"Si, it is me. What I'm going to do? I no have my rosary. I got to have it. Muy importante. You are Catholic. You understand? It is a special one, blessed by the Bishop, I got to have it with me."

Christine mouthed a, "What is it?"

As much as Annie dreaded it, she told her. "It's Mrs. Olmos. She lost her rosary."

Now was the perfect time for Chris to say I told you so, and she wasted no time in getting that little chore done, complete with a full eye roll.

"Mrs. Olmos, could you hold on just a minute?"

"Nurse, you gonna help me, si?"

"Yes, I just need to give someone a quick message."

"Annie, you know that rosary is probably long gone, what are you going to do? I've got to get home." A shake of her downturned head, as if Chris were dealing with a disobedient child, made Annie feel even worse.

"Look, you go on home, it's my fault. I am going to at least look for it. But I don't want you to stay, really."

"Are you going to go through all the dirty linen?" Even though Christine was righteously irritated, part of her still felt sorry for Annie.

"Chris, don't worry about me, I'll be okay. See you in the morning."

Christine slowly turned away and walked towards the dressing room. Annie returned to the waiting Mrs. Olmos.

"OK, Mrs. Olmos. Let me see. Did you have the rosary after surgery, do you remember?"

"No…I don't think so. Maybe I did. Can you look for it now, please?"

Annie assured her she would look for it and call her back either way. First, she started the easier way. Searching all the nooks and crannies in the recliner where Mrs. Olmos had sat brought no results. Ah, well now

36

to the yuckier part. She went back to the dirty linen room. As she pushed the door open, it seemed to push back at her, willing her not to come any farther. When she finally did get in, she saw that a large dirty laundry bag had fallen from a sizable mountain of bags and landed against the door, almost successfully preventing her from entering. Already she felt an adversarial relationship with these anonymous bags of dirty linen. There seemed to be no logical way to decide where to begin, so after putting on a pair of gloves she started with the bag closest to her. Of course, that bag produced no rosary. After the fourth bag, she contemplated admitting defeat. Mrs. Olmos had no idea how many laundry bags were here. She had given it a more than reasonable effort. Christine had been right all along, as much as Annie hated to admit it. Suddenly she remembered the story of Horton the Elephant and his persistence in finding the speck of dust that contained *Whoville* on the three millionth flower of his search. This memory encouraged her to dig through one more bag and, as if Horton's spirit were standing by, she found the rosary.

Calling Mrs. Olmos, she wished at least all this trouble could have been for a patient that she liked a little better.

"You found it? Thank you mucho, nurse, you bring it to mi casa?"

"Well, Mrs. Olmos, it's getting kind of late. Do you live close to the hospital? Maybe you could come get it tomorrow."

Long hesitation. "Nurse, I guess so. I really wanted it tonight to go to sleep with, but si, I can come tomorrow. I won't sleep so good without it."

Sigh. At this point Annie conceded defeat and got into the rosary delivery mode. She felt better when she heard the address carefully spelled out to her. "Oh, that's okay. I know where that street is. I can drop it off on my way home. I'll see you in a little while."

Calling Ben to let him know she was running late, she was met with his usual response when Annie was driving in unknown territory. "Annie, are you sure you can find it? You know how you are with directions."

"Yes, Ben, I am sure. I grew up in the neighborhood near this street. I remember it, no problem. I'll see you in thirty minutes or so. Bye."

As she turned down Bellfort, things looked different from her child-hood. She didn't recall so many places along the way that had big truck tires painted yellow with the words "flats fixed here" sitting prominently near the curb. There seemed to be more blue and purple houses than she remembered, and almost all the houses had burglar bars caging them. It did change one's bearing and she breathed a small sigh when she saw the street sign announcing Idaho come into view. The little frame house sat slightly tilted and unlike its' colorful neighbors, it was a dull grey/white, paint coming off like skin in a bad sunburn. She pulled into the driveway, noting another set of tires setting on the edge of the yard. Where do all these tires come from? She wondered absentmindedly. Surprisingly there was a pretty little flower bed right by the front door filled with blooming pink and purple petunias, made even more beautiful by the contrast of the dull surroundings.

The ringing doorbell must have roused a sleeping guard dog, from the frightening growls and barking that sent vibrations through the door (which Annie now noticed was rather flimsy indeed). The door opened and the quiet little man who was Mr. Olmos simply stood there looking at her as if she were a girl scout with cookies to sell. The dog directly behind his legs emitted a constant low growl and Annie wanted to simply set the rosary on the doorsill and quietly back away to the safety of her car. Unsure if putting a rosary on the ground might be sacrilegious, she decided against it.

"Hi, I'm Annie. Is this the Olmos home? I have Mrs. Olmos' rosary, see?"

She dangled it gently before her, which seemed to agitate the pit bull and be seen as a possible sign of aggression. He lunged and the screen bulged, on the verge of bursting.

A voice from farther in the house called out, " Nurse, is that you? Let her in Armando, don't make her stand outside."

" Oh, that's alright, it's getting late. If I could just give you this rosary here . . ."

Too late. The door opened fully to allow Annie inside and coincidentally to give the pit bull complete access to her. But Mr. Olmos, who still hadn't spoken, gave the dog a gentle tap on the head and instantly the dog became quiet.

" Mrs. Olmos, I hope this helps you to sleep better tonight. Well, I'll be leaving now. Goodnight."

" Nurse, come here, why you in such a hurry? What your name is please, I'm sorry I forgot."

"Oh, that's okay, you had a lot of other people and things to think about. My name is Annie and, well . . ."

"That's right. Annie, that's a nice name. You were the one who brought me a fresh Coke. Thank you, it tasted so much better. I didn't say thank you before."

"You're welcome, no problem. Are you drinking plenty of fluids? That's important, you know."

"Si, Armando brings me a coke every few minutes, I think." Here Armando came over and stood beside his wife, looking down with tender concern.

That's just how Ben would take care of me. "Looks like you've got a good nurse, Mrs. Olmos."

Mrs. Olmos reached out her hand towards Annie drawing her near with the gesture. She grasped Annie's hand and said, " I've got two good nurses, Annie. Thank you mucho mucho for finding my rosary and bringing it home to me. You got a good heart, I think."

"Well . . . I hope so, Mrs. Olmos. Thank you. I really need to get home now. I have a sweet husband waiting for me too."

"Oh, yes, Annie, that's good. Here, you take some fajitas and beans and tortillas home to your sweet husband. We all cooked yesterday so everything fresh."

"Thanks, but I better not. You have a big family that will be over soon, I bet."

"Annie, you no like fajitas and beans?"

"Yes, Mrs. Olmos, I actually do. I like them a lot."

" Annie, take them. You got to learn to take, not just give all the time. Armando . . ." But Armando had already quietly gone into the kitchen and was carefully wrapping food in foil and putting the beans in a big pickle jar, screwing the lid on carefully.

Annie decided that Mrs. Olmos' simple philosophy about learning to take as well as give was very true. In this case, it was also very tasty. Armando had carefully packed everything into a cardboard box and even put in a few napkins. What a sweet touch from this silent little man.

As Annie drove home, she decided to revise her opinions. Number one and most important – Christine was not right after all. Annie had an authentic Mexican meal sitting piping hot in her car. Take that, Christine! Of course, the fact that Annie had to dig through five bags of dirty linen to get it seemed to have escaped her at the moment. Number two – Mrs. Olmos was not the ungrateful grouch Annie had thought. She was a very kind lady who was just scared.

When Annie got home at 7:30 PM, getting out of the car she remembered something. She had never taken the safety in-service exit test. So much for personal responsibility.

3

MEMORANDUM

STATUS: PRIORITY
TO: ALL MEDICAL STAFF, ALL HOSPITAL PERSONNEL, AND DEPTS.
FROM: ADMINISTRATION
SUBJECT: OAT UNIT OPENING
OOPS! OUR SLIP IS SHOWING. IT HAS COME TO OUR ATTENTION THAT THE NEW OAT UNIT WAS OPENED PRIOR TO THE ANNOUNCEMENT TO THE MEDICAL STAFF AND OTHER HOSPITAL DEPTS. OUR APOLOGIES TO ALL! THE NEW UNIT IS OAT (OBSERVATION, ASSESS, TRANSFER). NURSE MANAGER: NITA STROMEYER, RN. IT IS LOCATED ON THE SECOND FLOOR WHERE THE OLD SLEEP LAB USED TO BE. IT IS AN OVERFLOW UNIT FOR DAY SURGERY AS WELL AS HOLDING AREA FOR PATIENTS WAITING FOR ADMISSION, DISCHARGE, OR TRANSFER. OPEN HOUSE WILL BE HELD IN 2 WEEKS. FURTHER MEMO WILL BE SENT. THANK YOU.

Six-fifteen the next morning found a bleary-eyed group of nurses gathered around a large long desk jutting out into the middle of the hallway on the new unit. Down both sides of the hallway randomly spaced were metal foldout stands, each of which held a computer. They gave the impression of being added as an afterthought. The overall appearance was one of a unit designed by a carpenter on heavy doses of mind-altering medication. But appearances were the least of the OAT unit issues. Nita stood at the center of the group, accompanied by Janet.

"Welcome everyone to the new OAT unit," Nita said in a grand fashion. "A concise and catchy name, don't you think? It stands for: Observation, Assessment and Transfer so I think that gives the unit a clear purpose."

To Annie, it seemed just one more confusing name for patients to try to understand in the vast maze of hospital terminology. Then again, no one had asked her.

Nita continued, "There are no positions in the budget to staff these units yet so until we get it up and going, we are going to ask the Day Surgery staff to FLOAT over here and work."

Annie thought of the book she was going to write one day titled, *Words That Mean Something Completely Different in the World of Nursing*. Not too concise or catchy, but accurate. One of the first words in the book would be: FLOATING. In the normal world, floating implied freedom like a feather in the gentle wind. The word in the language of nursing meant just the opposite. It was a mandatory, non-negotiable action. It meant being sent to work in another unit where there was a shortage of nurses. It meant, too, that the floatee often got the crummy assignment with the sickest patients. Nobody liked to float. Ever. Annie returned from her reverie to hear Christine bringing up an issue, in her usual bull-like fashion.

"There are no wheelchairs. You forgot to order wheelchairs."

Nita answered, "I didn't forget them. They are not budgeted. Plus you don't need them. Just call Transportation when you need one."

"That won't work because . . ." Christine began her defense.

"I notice there seems to be some negativity this morning and I'm not going to tolerate it. I make the necessary decisions on what I order based on the budget and necessity. What I need is a little more team spirit and willingness to make this new unit work. Any more questions?"

Well, no, surprisingly enough, no more questions.

The meeting broke up abruptly and people began scattering quickly to get morning tasks started. As Annie turned to go, Nita called out.

"Anna, could I speak to you a moment?"

"Sure, what's up?"

"Janet just told me this morning there was an incident of a missing rosary. I understand you found it and actually drove over to the patient's home to return it to her."

"Oh, yes, Mrs. Olmos. Well, it was very, very important to her and I just couldn't say no. I am willing to take responsibility . . ." Annie thought she might need a well thought-out defense. This early in the morning, she didn't have a well thought-out defense.

But Nita went on, "Oh, Anna, I'm not upset. I think it was a very kind and caring thing to do. I'm a Catholic, as you must be too (here a quiet conspiratorial look with meaningful eye contact at Annie), and I know how much I need my rosary at certain times. I just wanted to commend you."

"Why, thank you Nita. I appreciate that." It was so nice to have Nita like her that Annie couldn't bring herself to confess her non-Catholic status. Nita could be pretty if she tried at all. Her brown hair was pulled into a severe bun at the nape of her neck, not flattering to any face shape. But her eyes were a dark brown and at this moment had softness to them. The lips that were so often drawn into a thin line actually had a nice shape if she would just use a little lipstick to accent them.

Nita was continuing, "It's always important to recognize a patient's spiritual needs as well as the physical ones, and not everyone does that."

"Well, we are supposed to treat the whole patient and I try to . . ."

"By the way, Anna, you did all this off the clock, right? Because, I mean, overtime would never be approved for something like this."

"Yes, it was on my time, no problem." *It was nice while it lasted.*

"Good, I needed to be sure. The budget, you know. Have a nice day, Anna." With a faint squeak of her thick rubber-soled nursing shoes on the tile floor, she pivoted and was gone.

After the first of the morning's patients had all gone back to surgery, there was a brief lull. Annie told Christine she was going to pop over to ICU to check on Mrs. Nguyen. She put on her most assertive persona to get into ICU without being stopped by the authoritative ward clerk, who could have easily had a second career as a maximum security prison guard. Walking briskly, making no eye contact, and not speaking were key to getting in without a hassle. This morning she must have been putting out unusually assertive vibes because she arrived at Mrs. Nguyen's bedside easily.

Mrs. Nguyen looked up and gave Annie a big smile, lips pink, and no tinge of grey to her skin. There was no supplemental oxygen; she was doing fine just breathing room air.

"Hi, Mrs. Nguyen, you are looking good." Annie gave the universal thumbs up signal along with a big smile. Mrs. Nguyen seemed to understand, for she reached out and took Annie's hand. There wasn't much more Annie could do to communicate with this sweet little lady. She held her hand a moment longer, and then said what was probably just gibberish to Mrs. Nguyen.

"I've got to get back to work now. You are going to do okay, Mrs. Nguyen. Bye, bye."

Mrs. Nguyen nodded her head as if she understood every word, which Annie seriously doubted. She gently released her hold on her and Annie quietly exited. On the way out, her assertive persona must have faded somewhat. The ward clerk/prison guard spoke out loudly from her station at the desk, "Hey, this is not visiting hours, you know. You are supposed to check in at the desk." But with her mission accomplished, Annie could afford to be gracious.

"Oh, I'm sorry, I'm from Day Surgery. I just wanted to check on her. Thanks a lot!" And with a big smile and good eye contact she breezed out the door.

■ ■ ■

A couple of days later, Janet appeared at the desk where Annie and Christine sat working on charts.

"Hey, here are two of my favorite nurses," she said with a big smile.

Uh-Oh.

"The Oat Unit is going to open tomorrow at 6:00 AM. You and Christine will be the first two to float there. I want you to know I picked you because you are so FLEXIBLE and such a good team."

FLEXIBLE – another term Annie would put in her book about words and their meaning in the world of nursing. Whenever someone, especially a supervisor, came to Annie and started the conversation with, "Oh, there you are, one of my most flexible people" Annie knew that she was going to be asked to go to a unit she didn't want to go to, work a shift she didn't want to work, or be on some committee that nobody else would be on.

That afternoon, the charts were caught up and ready early for a change.

"Chris, let's walk over to the OAT unit and take a quick look-see."

"Good idea, Annie. I don't want to get blamed for not knowing where things are."

Annie wasn't very optimistic that a walk-through could prevent that, but didn't say anything to discourage Christine's hopes.

As they checked out the pantry in the new unit, they were surprised but glad to see the old blanket warmer from Day Surgery sitting in the corner.

"Look, they got Old Faithful over here. What do you know?"

When patients were nervous or shaky or cold, there was nothing as comforting as a warm blanket. Day Surgery had recently acquired a newer, modern blanket warmer, and must have loaned Old Faithful to the OAT, which otherwise would have been without one.

Old Faithful had both good and bad qualities. She was all dented, scratched up, and looked like a machine from the early 1900's. She may well have been. She was a metal rectangular box about three feet tall with one lone knob on the front control panel numbered one to ten. The door swung open from the front, revealing an all-metal interior, which, on number ten, could heat blankets almost to the point of scorching. A can of Campbell's soup placed in the back at 9:30 or so in the morning would produce piping hot soup when lunchtime rolled around. Of course this practice was strictly forbidden, although Annie could never understand how a can of soup could contaminate blankets and was one who occasionally broke this rule. Patients loved the toasty hot blankets that were produced. The funny thing was that Old Faithful wasn't built to be a blanket warmer, according to the maintenance man. Nobody knew exactly what she was designed to heat. Everybody just knew she always worked when the knob was turned up to ten. Her one drawback was that the inside of the metal front door heated up almost to the glowing point. If the front door was swung open too vigorously, it had a tendency to swing back. If it made contact with an arm reaching in to get a hot blanket, it would leave a red linear blister – a tattoo of sorts. In spite of being warned, all new personnel eventually sported the telltale blister mark until learning to properly respect Old Faithful. Annie remembered getting her introductory blister from Old Faithful several years ago.

Old Faithful, with her missing thermostat and ancient wiring, was not compliant with the current electrical safety guidelines. When the shiny new blanket warmer arrived, complete with safety coated doors and working thermostat, Old Faithful was relegated to the storage room. Old Faithful was, however, a force to be reckoned with. More than once the new modern blanket warmer would blow a fuse or quit working and the nurses would call maintenance to retrieve Old Faithful from storage. She would once again be turned on to ten and heat toasty blankets while her temperamental replacement was being repaired.

As Annie and Christine were leaving the unit to return to Day Surgery, they saw Nita standing in the pantry. She seemed to be staring at Old Faithful in deep thought. Annie and Christine quickly walked on, their nursing shoes moving in near silence down the hallway. However, Christine's left knee had a marked pop and marred the attempt at a stealthy exit, sounding as though a small toy pistol was being repeatedly fired. But Nita never looked up.

The next morning they met in the dressing room, changed into scrubs, and walked to the OAT to be ready for the first patients. Much to their surprise, when they arrived there was already activity on the unit. A nurse was sitting at the desk with papers strewn about and there were some patients already in the rooms.

"Hi, we're from Day Surgery. What's going on? We were supposed to open the unit this morning."

The nurse, who Annie didn't know, looked up and said, "I'm trying to get through here, give me a minute."

That meant, "Don't start talking to me and asking questions until I'm ready to talk."

Annie and Christine just looked at each other in silence. Shortly, the unknown nurse finished writing and stood up.

"Well, I'm out of here. This unit is a mess."

"Wait a minute, we need a report," Christine said. They had no idea who these patients were or what the situation was.

"All the beds in the hospital are full and there are four patients that came through ER last night and had to be admitted, so they put them here."

"We are supposed to be a Day Surgery overflow unit, not ER overflow patients."

"I just work here, okay? Did you want a report or not? Room one is an emphysema patient, he's better now. He should be going to a room on the medical floor as soon as one opens up. Room two is a chest pain, but he's not in any pain anymore, they think it's a pulled muscle or something. He'll probably be discharged as soon as his doctor comes by. Room three has a deep laceration of the hand, cut it on a saw or something. He may have to have surgery to repair it, I don't know. Room four is a SOB. (This was not a derogatory term, but medical shorthand for "shortness of breath".) He has O2 going and is sleeping. I'm out of here."

Picking up her canvas carry-all bag with a half-eaten bag of Fritos protruding, she exited without another word leaving Annie and Christine standing openmouthed. Clipboards lay scattered about on the desk.

"She didn't even give us their names. That was a terrible report," Christine's words spoken too loudly betrayed her irritation. There was nothing to be done but start assessing these patients and trying to figure things out.

"I'll take one and two, you take three and four. Is that okay, Chris?"

Annie proceeded to room one. She was met by sounds of wheezing that she could hear easily as soon as she entered. If this patient was better now, he must have really been in acute respiratory distress on admission. He looked pale, lips a little grey even with oxygen going. His name was Mr. Camp. His eyes met hers as she entered and she recognized the look in them – fear. He wasn't getting enough oxygen.

"Hi, Mr. Camp. I'm Annie, one of the nurses. You look like you are having some trouble breathing."

He couldn't even answer. It took too much effort so he just nodded his head.

She quickly checked his vital signs and felt his skin, which was ice cold and wet with perspiration. Turning up the oxygen flow, she knew he needed more than that but maybe it would help a little until she could get him some medicine.

"I'm going to give your doctor a call and see if we can give you a breathing treatment. I'll be right back, okay?"

His only answer was another nod of his head.

Annie went to the phone and asked that Mr. Camp's doctor be paged. If she was lucky, maybe he was in the building already. That apparently wasn't the case because he didn't respond.

Putting in a call to the answering service, Dr. Nagel was surprisingly quick to return the page.

"What's the problem, Annie?"

"Mr. Camp, your patient in room one, is still really wheezy and short of breath, looks in distress, could we give him a breathing treatment?"

"Yes, get an albuterol treatment now and repeat the chest x-ray afterwards. He's in the ER room one, you said? I told them to admit him to the floor."

"Sir, he's in the OAT unit, room one, waiting for a hospital bed to open up."

"What's that?"

Annie upped the volume of her voice to continue, "I said, 'he's in the OAT unit, waiting . . .'"

"No, no, I heard you. What is the OAT unit?"

"It is supposed to be an overflow unit for Day Surgery, but I guess the hospital is totally full so we have your patient and three others from ER."

"Where is this unit? Why wasn't I told about it?" Sounds of irritation filtering through on the phone were signs of a ruffling of the giant ego of the good doctor.

"Dr. Nagel, I'm sorry, I thought there would have been a memo to all the docs. It is on the second floor where the sleep lab used to be. Do you know where that is?"

"Yes, I remember. I'll be over in a few minutes. Get that breathing treatment stat. "

"Yes sir, right away. Bye," Annie hung up the phone, irritated at Dr. Nagel's tone. After all, she was the one who had called HIM.

Paging respiratory therapy, Annie shouldn't have been surprised at the therapist's response.

"The OAT unit, what's that?"

"It's on the second floor where the sleep lab used to be. The patient really needs a treatment stat. Thanks."

"Hey, be sure and put the order in on the computer, would you, Annie?"

"I'll do that now. See you in a minute." First, though, Annie went in to check on her patient.

"Mr. Camp, respiratory therapy is on the way to give you a breathing treatment."

Mr. Camp nodded in approval. His face seemed to relax just a little, as if reassured that someone was taking care of him.

"I'll come back in just a minute. I have to put the order in the computer. You know that computers rule," Annie nodded with a quick smile as she walked away. Entering an order in the computer generally was not a complicated procedure but this was not an ordinary day. Each patient was located by his bed number and try as she might, the OAT beds didn't seem to be anywhere in the computer.

"Chris, come here a minute. This is weird. I can't enter this order."

Although Annie considered herself to be a pretty independent nurse, she didn't hesitate to call for help when it came to the computer. It seemed to sense her fear and discomfort and deliberately not function when she was at the keyboard. Chris, on the other hand, projected a sense of power and the computer knew when it was beaten. It would meekly progress to the correct screen after she stepped in. Christine usually said something to Annie like, "How in the world did you get to this screen?" Comments like that did nothing to foster Annie's fragile confidence in her computer abilities.

Chris, for once, was stymied too. "Why aren't the OAT beds listed anywhere? What's going on here?" She fiddled around a little more while Annie looked on helplessly. Meanwhile, the respiratory therapist arrived at the unit and Annie directed her to Mr. Camp.

What the proper treatment could do to help a patient in respiratory distress was always surprising. Within just five minutes of finishing his treatment, the wheezes had subsided and Mr. Camp managed a little smile at Annie. She took his vital signs again which were greatly improved. His skin wasn't cold and clammy anymore.

"Where's my coffee and breakfast, girl?"

Annie knew then that Mr. Camp was better for sure. Asking for morning coffee was a good sign.

Where was breakfast, anyway? The trays should have been here by now. Annie let the respiratory therapist know she couldn't get the order entered on the computer for reasons unknown and handed her a universal requisition. This was the backup system for handling computer problems or down time. It was a piece of actual paper, hand written the good old-fashioned way, which Annie could manage quite nicely, thank you.

Meanwhile, Chris had problems of her own. Her patient in room three with the hand injury was supposed to go to x-ray at 7:00 AM. Chris had stumbled on the orders in her usually thorough manner, reviewing both her patients' charts meticulously. (Annie realized she hadn't looked in either of her patient charts yet). The patient was feeling shaky and didn't want to walk to x-ray. Chris needed a wheelchair. The problem was that the transportation department didn't open until 7:30. X-ray needed the patient now.

"This was just what I was trying to tell Nita but no, she knows everything. This makes me so mad! I'll be late getting that patient to x-ray. Where could I get a wheelchair quick?"

"Call Day Surgery. I bet somebody would run one over."

Annie had been tied up with Mr. Camp and hadn't had a chance to check her other patient. His call light lit up before she could get to the room. As she entered, she was met with an irritated, "There you are! When am I getting out of this place? There's nothing the matter with me." The patient, a forty-year-old type A personality if Annie ever saw one, was sitting up, dangling his legs on the side of the bed and was in the process of pulling off the tape that attached his IV.

"Mr. Flinn, wait, don't take that out yet, please!"

"Well, you take it out then. The doctor in the emergency room told me I could go home in the morning and if I'm not mistaken, the sun is up." It took everything Annie could muster to coax Mr. Flinn into waiting for her to check his vital signs.

"The doctor ordered one more EKG this morning, just to be sure everything is still negative."

"Well, get it done! Let's get going!"

"The EKG technician should be here in just a few minutes. How about some breakfast?" Maybe food would distract him.

Mr. Flinn agreed to eat before discontinuing his IV and leaving.

Annie left to check on the trays. There were none in sight. She was sure they should have been here by now. Better call the kitchen.

A call determined that not only were the trays late, there were no meals ordered for this unit. Annie was met with the now familiar question, "The OAT unit, what is that?" After explaining what and where it was, she was told the diet orders would have to be entered in the computer before food could be sent. After pleading with the head dietician, that requirement was temporarily waived.

Meanwhile, Christine had discovered another problem. None of the patients had been given any medication. No breathing medicine, no heart medicine, no antibiotics had been started. Since this unit was supposed to be a Day Surgery overflow, it was not equipped with a standard medication room, just a small alcove with a counter and a locked medicine cabinet with pain and anti-nausea medications. It looked like the night nurse had simply ignored the medication orders, using the logic, "No medication room---no medicines."

Chris called the pharmacy to explain the situation and faxed the orders for the medicines. Unfortunately, a large snag was hit at this point. The pharmacy technician said it was illegal for her to send medicines to a patient that had no location in the computer. At this point, the volume of Chris' voice went up a few notches and there was a desperate quality to it that Annie had not noticed earlier. She recognized all the signs, having worked with Christine for years, and took action. She paged Janet. Although Janet wasn't really in charge of this unit, Annie knew she would do something to fix the situation.

Janet accurately assessed the situation immediately. "That is terrible, the patients not getting any medication all night. I'll call the Pharmacy manager and see what I can do. You need to make out an incident report, Annie. This is a medication error."

"Right, Janet, I'll get to it later on." Janet was a great manager but she was sometimes overly focused on paper work. Not only did Annie not have the time or inclination right now to fill out an incident report, she had no idea of where the forms were located in this odd unit.

For once, things happened at a brisk pace. Within the hour, four white medication bags were hand-delivered to the OAT unit. As there was no secure medication room, Annie and Chris decided to line them up in the center of the big desk. The four white paper bags gave the desk a lunchroom type ambience.

As if on cue to continue this weird morning, Dr. Nagel came strolling into the unit.

"So this is the OAT unit. Not much to it, is there?"

Inwardly, Annie couldn't have agreed with him more, but she didn't want to be accused of negativity so she just mumbled something about how it was not supposed to be a big unit and it being the opening day, there were some kinks to work out. She accompanied Dr. Nagel to see Mr. Camp who was looking much better by this time.

"Oh, hi, Doc. How's everything? You need to give this little girl here a raise. She got me all straightened out, didn't you, honey?"

Sometimes being called a "little girl" and "honey" in the same sentence was irritating to Annie but this wasn't one of those times. Mr. Camp was just being appreciative, not demeaning; and to him, she may have seemed like a little girl since he was seventy-five.

Dr. Nagel listened to Mr. Camp's lungs and seemed to agree with his patient.

"Maybe we will get her a little raise, Mr. Camp." He even gave Annie a rare smile. "You should be getting a room anytime now. If you don't have any more problems today, I'll send you home in the morning with some new breathing medications."

"Great, Doc. I just have one little complaint. I'm still waiting for breakfast."

"Annie is going to take care of that for you, I'm sure. Aren't you, Annie?"

"There was a mix-up because the kitchen didn't know about the OAT unit either. The trays are supposed to be on the way up, but I'll check on it for you, Mr. Camp. I promise I will get you something to eat, if I have to go to the cafeteria myself."

With that guarantee, Mr. Camp smiled. "Thanks, honey."

By 8:15 the breakfast trays had arrived and Mr. Camp and Mr. Flinn were temporarily distracted. Annie knew that right after breakfast, one way or another, Mr. Flinn would have his IV out and be ready to go.

The phone rang with a call from the hospital recovery room. They had a patient to bring to the unit for progressive recovery and discharge. Mrs.

Moore was a thirty-two year old lady who had just had a breast biopsy. She was drowsy but stable.

Momentarily, the stretcher rolled into the unit. Annie and Chris both went to assist getting the patient settled. Mrs. Moore was shivering so badly that her teeth were chattering.

"I don't know why I'm so cold," she looked up with concern.

"Her temp is normal," the recovery nurse said. "It's some of the anesthesia medicine that makes you shivery, Mrs. Moore, it'll wear off in a few minutes."

"We'll get you some warm blankets, Mrs. Moore. They will help, too," Annie said, walking to the pantry to pick some up. Much to her surprise, the old blanket warmer was nowhere to be seen.

"Well, I'll be. Where in the world did that thing go?"

As she walked out of the pantry, she almost ran into Nita.

"Hi, Nita. Do you know what happened to the blanket warmer that was here yesterday?"

"That old thing? It looked awful. I don't want anything that junky on my new unit. I had it moved to storage."

"What are we supposed to do for warm blankets?" Annie asked, in puzzlement.

"Borrow some from the hospital recovery room, if you ever need any."

"But Nita, we can't be leaving the unit every time we need a warm blanket."

"Sounds like you may have caught some of Christine's negative attitude, Anna. We all may have to be a little inconvenienced at times, but you have to adapt and be flexible to make things work. No other complaints?"

Annie was so angry she didn't trust herself to speak. It was a good thing, because Nita had already turned and begun walking away.

Annie returned to Mrs. Moore's room where Chris was still checking her in.

"Where are the blankets, Annie? She really needs them."

"There's a little problem with the blanket warmer. I am going to run over to the main recovery room and grab some. I'll be right back." Annie did not want to tell Chris the true nature of the blanket warmer problem in front of a patient.

Within five minutes Mrs. Moore was cocooned in warm blankets and comfortable. At the desk, Annie told Chris the story. "You won't believe this, Chris. Nita had the blanket warmer shipped back to storage because it was too "junky looking" so we are supposed to borrow any blankets we need from the main recovery room."

"That is totally damn ridiculous," Christine blurted out, so loudly that Annie was sure patients had heard. She glanced towards the patient rooms and saw several startled looks toward the desk where she and Christine sat.

"Chris, not so loud, I'm fixing to call Janet" Annie responded softy. Inwardly though, she thought that Chris' assessment had "hit the nail on the head", as her Dad would have said.

"Janet, I know you are technically not the manager of this unit, but you have to do something about Nita. Already we couldn't get the medications, we couldn't get food for the patients, can't get them in the computer still, and now I go back to get a warm blanket and Nita has moved the old blanket warmer back to storage. 'It's too junky' according to her. She suggested I leave the unit and go to the main recovery room if I needed any. I've just about had it with her."

"Tell her I've had it too," Christine piped in, with a voice that carried all over the unit.

Janet firmly replied, "Tell Christine she's yelling and to calm down. I'll talk to Nita. She probably just didn't realize how often you need warm blankets. I'm sending Teresa over to assist until things settle down some, will that help?"

"Yeah, thanks. We are pretty fed up over here."

Chris quieted down after Annie's reassurances and with the news that Teresa was coming over. Annie suddenly thought about Mr. Flinn, her patient in room two. As she went into his room, he was standing with his back to her, fully dressed. When he turned around she saw his arm. He had obviously removed the IV, but didn't know to put pressure on the puncture site. As a result there was a huge hematoma and he had managed to get some blood on his pants.

"Mr. Flinn, let me look at that. You kind of made a mess of things." Mr. Flinn was not in the mood to be criticized and pulled his arm back as Annie approached.

"I told you I was going home after breakfast and you didn't come back so I'm handling things myself."

Yes, my life as a diva is so time-consuming, plus you are the only person in the world and should never have to wait on anything or anyone for any reason.

"Look, Mr. Flinn, I'm sorry I didn't get right back to you. I'll go put in a call to your doctor right now and see when he's coming by. I'll tell him you are anxious to go."

"I AM going. I'm not 'anxious to go'. I have things to do today." Sometimes it seemed to Annie that she couldn't say anything right.

"You tell him if he can't be here in fifteen minutes, I'm leaving."

" Mr. Flinn, but if you leave before the doctor discharges you it's called leaving AMA – against medical advice – and I just need to warn you sometimes your insurance won't pay, I've been told."

"You just call the doctor and let me worry about the insurance." Mr. Flinn was not in the least concerned with Annie's warning.

As Annie approached the desk, Teresa walked up.

"Hey, how's every little thing, Annie? Boy, this is pretty small," Teresa remarked in her ever-present cheery tone, looking around the strange little unit Annie was growing to hate. But Teresa was just the person Annie wanted to see.

"Teresa, could you go in room two and see if you can keep that patient from leaving AMA until I can get his doctor? He is a true type A, and he is pretty irritable right now."

As totally frustrated as Annie was, she had to stop and shake her head in admiration as Teresa turned up her schmooze factor to maximum strength.

"Why, honey, what in the world have you done to your arm? Oh my goodness, let me fix that for you. Oh, and look, there is some blood that got on your pants. Let me put some cold water on that so the stain doesn't set in. Boy those are nice looking pants, and your shirt just matches. Do you pick out your own clothes? If you do, you have a great color sense."

The poor guy never knew what hit him. Teresa had him sitting down as she carefully applied a clean dressing over his bloody IV site and cleaned the blood stains from his pants at the same time, million-dollar smile flashing all the while.

Mr. Flinn sat there as meekly as a little lamb. It really was something to watch Teresa at work.

Meanwhile, Annie had gotten Mr. Flinn's doctor on the phone. He was well aware of Mr. Flinn's type A personality. Fortunately, he was on his way up to the OAT unit after getting instructions on:

1. What it was.
2. How to find it.

As Annie went to Mr. Flinn's room to let him know the doctor was on the way, he and Teresa were laughing together and he seemed to have had a complete personality transplant in addition to getting the blood stains removed from his pants. The difficult patient answered in an unbelievably mellow tone when Annie told him the news.

"That's fine, nurse, and thank you. I can wait a little longer."

Annie walked out of his room in wonder. As she looked up, approaching the desk were the CEO of the hospital, Mr. Evans, accompanied by the Vice President of Nursing, Jayne Johnson. Although Annie and Christine had only met the V.P. of Nursing one other time, she greeted them both by name, as if they all met for coffee every morning.

"Annie and Christine, so good to see you two. Mr. Evans and I wanted to come by and personally express our thanks to you for being so FLEXIBLE and willing to help out in our bed crunch."

If this was an opportunity for honesty, Annie had gone into her smiling coward mode and heard words come out that had never entered her mind before, "We are glad to help out." Christine just nodded her head, her mouth remarkably closed, giving no indication of her previous opinion so loudly expressed just a few moments ago.

"We are working on getting some open beds so hopefully by this evening the OAT unit will be back to being the OAT unit it was designed to be. Is there anything you need?"

"No, not really, thank you though. Everything is great," Annie continued in her best "team buddy" persona while Christine remained standing, statue-like, in full mute mode.

And just as quickly as they appeared, they were gone.

"You sure were chatty and happy. You sounded as though this was the best day in the world. What do you mean – everything is great?" Christine finally spoke.

"I knew it wouldn't do any good to complain. What about you – you never said one word."

Annie knew she had been a mealy-mouth chicken and would have really felt guilty except Christine's behavior – total silence – was no better. Christine stomped off muttering, "At least I didn't say everything was great."

But somehow they made it through the rest of the day. When they left at 6:30 PM there were still hospital patients in the OAT beds but a night nurse had come on to relieve them.

Annie came on duty the next morning feeling beaten down and defeated by the previous day's trials, but there was an unexpected bright spot when she entered the hallway of the OAT unit. As she walked past the pantry area a sparkle on dented metal caught her eye. Who was sitting there almost regally but Old Faithful, and as Annie turned the knob up to ten and loaded it up with blankets, she had to smile at the thought that Old Faithful had returned, triumphant again. As she walked toward the desk, she looked up to see Nita making her way toward her.

"Anna, could you come into the pantry for a minute? I need to speak with you privately."

No "hello," "good morning", or any other civil greeting gave Annie an uneasy feeling in the pit of her stomach as she followed Nita to the pantry. After turning to close the door, Nita faced her and her expression actually was a little scary.

"Let's get something straight here, Anna. You may not like me, but I am the manager of this unit. Get used to it. I will not tolerate insubordination in any fashion, ever. Do I make myself clear?"

"I'm sorry, Nita. I don't know what you are talking about," Annie answered back, being completely in the dark about what the heck was going on.

"Did I make a mistake yesterday? It was pretty hectic at times, with it being the first day and all . . ."

"Please don't bother putting on the innocent act with me. I can assure you I see right through you."

"Nita, you are obviously upset with me, but I really and truly do not know what I have done wrong."

"You decided that you knew more about the running of this unit than I do. You didn't like the fact that I had this piece of crap moved (here, she turned and pointed accusingly at Old Faithful, who seemed to have a contented glow, unaware of the insult just leveled at her). You weren't satisfied with my decision and you just thought you would call your buddy Janet and she would fix everything the way YOU wanted it, didn't you?"

A small shower of spittle moistened the air in Annie's direction. She heard Nita breathing deep, rapid sighs, as if she were preparing for an actual physical confrontation.

"Nita, I was just frustrated and I am used to calling Janet. I can see how you felt offended and I am truly sorry."

Memo to self — do not ever cross this woman again.

"Believe me; you do not want me for an enemy. I can make things unpleasant and . . . let's just leave it at that. I know your kind, and I don't like you, Anna. I am being upfront about it."

"Nita, all I know to say is that I am sorry." Annie was at a loss for words at this level of rage.

"Well, I believe we know where we both stand, so I imagine Christine can use some help right about now." Annie, who had gotten a general idea of "where we stand", remained motionless as Nita opened the door and walked out.

Annie felt shaky and would have liked nothing better than to run out the doorway, down the long hall back to the dressing room. There she would change and head straight for the car. From there, maybe she would drive down to the beach where she would sit and compose her letter of resignation which the next day Nita would accept amid gales of laughter. But Annie really did not have the luxury of time to plan her exit strategy, as there were two pre-op patients that needed to be assessed.

4

MEMORANDUM

STATUS: PRIORITY
SUBJECT: HANDLING RUMORS
TO: ALL HOSPITAL PERSONNEL
FROM: MR. EVANS, CEO
IT HAS COME TO MY ATTENTION THAT THERE ARE SEVERAL UPSETTING RUMORS BEING SPREAD AROUND THE HOSPITAL, WHICH ARE UNFOUNDED AND AFFECTING HOSPITAL MORALE. IF YOU ARE APPROACHED BY SOMEONE SPREADING ONE OF THESE RUMORS (OBVIOUSLY, I CAN'T BE SPECIFIC) IT IS SUGGESTED THAT YOU GO TO YOUR UNIT MANAGER FOR ACCURATE INFORMATION. THIS WILL EFFECTIVELY NEGATE THESE FRIGHTENING AND INCORRECT RUMORS.

After a two-week rotation to the OAT, Annie and Christine were finally returning to Day Surgery. A warm feeling of security and the certainty of knowing where things were surrounded Annie as she walked into pre-op. The tension in her neck seemed to have vanished. A glance at her overflowing mailbox reminded her accusingly that she hadn't checked it since being away. One memo caught her eye. It was from the infection control nurse, announcing to anyone who had cared for a certain Mrs. Nguyen, that this patient had tested positive for TB. Surprise, surprise, Dr. Nagel strikes again in his efforts to spread TB throughout the hospital. Poor Teresa -- she had probably had an anxiety attack when the memo came out. There were just two days left to meet the deadline for getting TB skin tests.

Janet rounded the corner and greeted Annie with a hug. "I know it was hard being the first ones to open the OAT unit, but I am sure that you and Christine did a fantastic job."

"It was pretty rough at first but it gradually got better. It is good to be back here, though. There was one thing that really bugged me, Janet. You remember the day I called you about the blanket warmer being removed?"

" Yes, it got put back, didn't it?"

"Umhum, we got it ok. I was just wondering – when you called Nita was she upset?"

"No, she said she appreciated me bringing the problem to her attention and it would be taken care of, why?"

"Well, she was really angry with me, I think, for calling you instead of her. She . . . "

"Annie, I'm sure she just had a lot on her mind. You probably got the wrong impression if she was a little curt."

"A little curt" was a pretty big understatement, in Annie's opinion.

"No, Janet, she doesn't like me. In fact she hates me and . . ."

"Annie, Nita doesn't hate you, I'm sure. You are being overly sensitive, which you are sometimes. Nita is very particular about how things are done. She always has been. She was in my class in nursing school, did you know that?"

"I sure didn't. Was she, well, weird or anything?"

"I wouldn't say weird, Annie. Nita has been through some pretty rough times in her life and it has had an effect on her, just like it would you, so . . ." Janet paused, at a loss for how to finish the sentence. Annie stood, nodding her head slightly, hoping that subtle cue would enter Janet's subconscious and encourage her forward to explain this sick behavior.

The moment was broken when Christine walked past bringing a patient back to check in and Janet lurched forward, like a racehorse from the starting blocks, following Christine down the hall, calling out a welcome back.

Annie put the pile of unread memos back in her mailbox for later. Now was no time to read mail. There were patients waiting. As she entered the waiting room, she was greeted by the noise of Mrs. Olmos and her family together in a friendly huddle.

"There my nurse," Mrs. Olmos called out with a wave of her hand, motioning Annie over.

"Why, hello, Mrs. Olmos. Good to see you! How are you?"

"Nurse, I got to have another little test. Will you take care of me?"

"Sure, Mrs. Olmos, I'll be glad to. Let me be sure there is an open room." Annie hurried back to pre-op to claim room six, the one large pre-op room. She knew the whole family would come back, so why not embrace that reality instead of fighting it?

Fortunately room six was vacant, so Annie walked out and with a sweeping gesture of her arm, welcomed the entire Olmos clan back. They looked a little surprised but quickly gathered up jackets and a few kids and trouped down the hall together, a small Hispanic invasion. Christine looked up from the desk with a stern expression, but Annie carefully avoided eye contact and said, "It's okay, I'm putting them in room six. I think it will cut down on the back and forth traffic if they are all together." She didn't wait for a response, feeling Christine's disapproval inching toward her as she walked past.

Mrs. Olmos was back to have a lymph node biopsy to determine if the melanoma had spread to other parts of her body. It was a small surgery with big consequences. If the biopsy results were negative, Mrs. Olmos' chances of survival were greatly improved. If there were cancer cells in the lymph nodes, it meant the cancer had spread. Invisible now, it was only a matter of time before they made their presence known.

"You stick me, nurse, not nobody else," Mrs. Olmos made her touching request as she held out her arm. It was a stark contrast of their first meeting. Annie started the IV with several sets of eyes watching protectively as she carefully taped it in place.

"I'll check on you after your surgery, Mrs. Olmos. Is there anything else you need now?"

Everyone seemed contented and even the little kids were amazingly under control.

The rest of the morning passed fairly uneventfully, with one small exception. Anita of the housekeeping staff told Annie she had heard that the hospital was running out of money. Annie had long ago thought that Housekeeping staff should all wear zippy little name badges with the slogan, "We get the news first, we get the news fast!" imprinted above their names. As they quietly went about their work cleaning every part of the hospital, from the office of the CEO to the public restrooms, they had an information network that the CIA would envy.

"What do you mean? Is the hospital going to close down, Anita?"

But Anita's source was not sure exactly what the information meant. And like the CIA, housekeeping did not respond well to pressure or additional questioning. "I don't know any more, Annie. I'll tell you when I do, okay?"

Annie had to be content with that vague warning until she could verify it. Later in the day, Janet stopped by the pre-op desk where Annie sat.

"I've been in meetings all day. I'm exhausted." All traces of lipstick were gone, which gave her a pale and tired appearance.

"Janet, I heard that the hospital is in financial trouble. Is there any truth to that or is that one of those rumors Mr. Evans was talking about?"

"Why are you asking about that?"

Why didn't she deny it? Not a good sign.

"Oh, I don't know, a little something called job security . . . like when we go to the time clock tomorrow to clock in, will it be removed and replaced with a memo telling us to turn in our name badges?" Ha, ha!

But Janet apparently did not see the humor in Annie's illustration. She turned away and walked towards Lee in Progressive Recovery.

Well, so much for getting accurate information from your unit manager as instructed by the anti-rumor memo.

The next afternoon, a new memo was taped to the message board by the time clock, for all to see as they got off duty. Upcoming mandatory meetings for all personnel with the CEO were announced. Without any further information as to the nature of these meetings rumors were sure to form, despite the anti-rumor memo.

There was a buzz of conversation in the dressing room as people were leaving. No one except Anita had heard anything to merit this kind of memo, so the main topic was the hospital financial state. Everyone knew of other hospitals in the city that had closed or been gobbled up by large for-profit hospital corporations. Annie had heard some unsettling stories about for-profit hospitals and hoped that was not what was coming.

The next morning at 6:00 AM Annie, Christine, Teresa, and Lee were sitting in dining room two with many other employees from different departments all over the hospital. Mr. Evans, the CEO, was at the back of the room, trying to make small talk, pretty unsuccessfully with some of the housekeeping staff.

He called the meeting to order and began explaining the financial crisis.

"There are several issues which have contributed to our present situation. Managed care has meant the HMO's cut back on what illnesses and procedures will be approved for hospitalizations. This, in turn, means that often folks who were sick enough to be hospitalized in times past are no longer covered for hospitalization. This means that patients who are hospitalized are much more ill, requiring intensive and expensive nursing care, as you folks know. Medicare has also cut the amount of money they will reimburse both the hospital and the doctor for certain procedures. Our budget has been getting tighter as the needs and expenses grow and the income decreases."

His voice droned on with more bad news. Surgeons were forming partnerships and opening privately owned surgicenters. The tendency was to funnel healthy patients with good insurance to the surgicenters. The surgeons who did the operations there then shared in the profit. What was left over was not as desirable. Patients with poor insurance or no insurance, or needing expensive procedures, were left for the hospital. This meant a very uneven distribution of the health care dollar, thus the term cherry-picking. Annie and the other nurses already knew many of these facts, but hearing them stated all together was very overwhelming. It made Annie wonder how she even got a paycheck every two weeks.

As if all that were not depressing enough, there was more news concerning Day Surgery. Several of the doctors had put together a proposal to buy it. A joint venture between the hospital and the doctors was under consideration. If the hospital didn't go for the deal, the doctors were threatening to take all their patients to other hospitals or to open up their own surgicenter.

Immediately, hands went up in the Day Surgery section bombarding Mr. Evans with questions. Ms. Johnson, the vice president of nursing, sat silently at his side looking like a cardboard cutout with a benign smile pasted on her face.

"Will we still be employees of the hospital? What about our benefits and seniority? Will our pay scale be the same?"

Mr. Evans' only response was, "Don't worry. The hospital will take care of it's nurses." This reassurance had roughly the comfort factor of being offered one last cigarette before the blindfold and then the last sound to ring in your ears – multiple gunshots as your body fell in a bloody heap to the ground, Annie reflected. The looks on the faces of the Day Surgery nurses were grim and tight as they left the meeting.

"What will happen to us? Should we start looking for another place to work?" Almost everyone was frightened and angry. There was always someone in the crowd who took the management line, which served only to add to the anger of the group.

"Mr. Evans is the CEO and if he said the hospital will take care of us, we should believe him," Trena, one of the younger nurses spoke up.

"Trena, please, get a grip on reality. Nobody in management is going to take care of you," Christine spoke what everyone else felt. Trena, sensing she was greatly outnumbered said no more.

As the next few weeks wore on, Annie, along with her co-workers, had to simply accept that this situation was out of her control. She had no way of bringing money to the hospital other than counterfeiting some and depositing it in the "Suggestions for Improvement" boxes scattered around the hospital. But everyone knew they were rarely if ever opened, so even that solution wouldn't have helped. Denial, one of Annie's usual defenses, went into critical level mode – *nothing will probably ever happen.* On good days this was easy. On bad days, and especially when another rumor would float by like a dark cloud, it was really hard. The uncertainty of their future slowly took a toll on them all. It ate away at peace of mind in little bits, and gradually people got more and more irritable at little things. Lack of job security was an unknown to most nurses, and they seemed ill-equipped to cope with it.

"Did you charge for that box of Kleenex you pulled?" Christine, in an accusing tone, questioned Annie as she was blowing her nose in pre-op one afternoon. The charge sticker sat visibly stuck to the Kleenex box as concrete evidence of Annie's guilt.

"I don't think one box of Kleenex is going to send the hospital into bankruptcy," Annie snapped back.

"Mr. Evans said that little charges mount up, and we have to all do our part. You drank one of the patient supply Cokes yesterday, too."

Annie realized she was enjoying pulling things off the supply cart and not charging for them. Of course, it would have to be Christine who would notice her immature behavior.

But there was more than one person with some strange ways of dealing with the tension. In progressive recovery, Lee had taken to sending patients home still too sedated, in an effort to improve the budget. But just yesterday, a patient was so dizzy he almost fell getting into the wheelchair. Annie could foresee someone falling and being injured, resulting in a million-dollar lawsuit, effectively negating Lee's early discharge budgeting plan. Cost of patient staying an extra hour to get fully awake: $200. Cost of lawsuit resulting from woozy patient falling out of wheelchair: $1,000,000.

Christine had uncharacteristically begged Annie to take this next patient. He had been scheduled a few weeks ago and never showed up. Annie wasn't in the best frame of mind to deal with a difficult patient, but he had chosen this particular day and time to appear at Day Surgery when scheduled so, resigned to facing him, she approached the check-in desk. As she called out his name, the raspy squeak of a wheel chair slowly rolling toward her was the only response.

"Mr. Allen?" Annie intoned again. The woman beside him, probably his wife, finally spoke a short "yes" when he rolled to a stop in front of her. His color had the peculiar pallor common to chronic kidney patients. His hair, thinning and coarse, was scraggly and uncombed. An old flannel shirt buttoned askew and wrinkled, stained khakis completed his wardrobe. It became obvious he hadn't bathed in a while as they entered Annie's zone of smelling. He was missing the lower part of his right leg, which explained the wheelchair.

"Hi, I'm Annie, your nurse. Come on back. Let's get you checked in and ready."

No response but a scowl and shake of his head.

His wife suddenly began talking, "His arm is real sore. That dialysis catheter got clogged up yesterday at the clinic. We're here to get it fixed. It's worked good for two years now but . . . but . . ."and then Mrs. Allen sputtered to a stop, like a car out of gas.

If Annie had to pick a particular type of patient NOT to take care of, it would be a dialysis patient. Because of being chronically ill, they had to endure a lot of pain and discomfort and were often termed difficult patients. They came to the hospital often, knew the routine, and they were sick of it.

"Mr. Allen, I need your temperature please."

"I don't see why you have to take my temperature. I'm here to get the catheter fixed. I don't have any fever." He then clamped his mouth shut and turned his head away from her in angry defiance.

Annie looked over to his wife for a little help but she had her eyes focused on the floor, as if in deep thought studying the pattern of the floor tile. Annie noticed Mr. Allen shivering and offered him a warm blanket. As she was wrapping it around him, she bumped his sore arm, causing a string of expletives to come from Mr. Allen ending with, "What in the hell are you trying to do, hurt me?"

Annie took a step back, the force of profanities like a physical slap. Wordless, she mouthed a silent prayer to be able to see this man as he truly was. As she continued to stare, it was as if his anger, fear, and pain became visible, wrapped about him like the blankets.

"Well, what are you looking at?" Mr. Allen glanced up towards Annie in disgust.

Annie crouched and knelt down beside him. At eye level she spoke softly, "Mr. Allen, are you looking for a fight?"

He didn't appear in the least surprised by her question, and answered without hesitation "yes", glaring directly into her eyes.

"Well, Mr. Allen, you picked the wrong person. I'm not going to fight with you. I know you are sick and tired of the hospital, so what can I do that will make it better for you?"

"Nothing, let's just get this thing over with."

"Well, okay then, the first thing we need is to get you changed into a hospital gown and . . ."

"Damn it, why? It hurts me to move and it took me an hour to get dressed."

Normally, patients are changed into a clean hospital gown to go to a sterile surgical room, especially when they have a grungy smell like Mr. Allen, but maybe Annie could bend the rules a little here.

"How about if I just take off your shirt and put a gown on, and you can leave your pants on and they'll take them off when you are lying down in the operating room?"

69

His expression softened just barely and he nodded a terse okay. Annie knew that the surgery nurse would not like this arrangement at all, but she was ready to take the heat for it.

The next hurdle was to get a blood specimen. She wasn't sure how this news would be received, but she had a pretty good idea.

"Don't you folks get tired of hurting people for no reason at all? It doesn't matter, my potassium is going to be high since I didn't have dialysis yesterday, what fricking difference does it make?"

By this time Annie was on a personal quest to try and make things better for this miserable old man. "Well, let me think, your procedure is being done over in the main hospital surgery today. How about if I call the hospital pre-op room and see if they can draw a blood sample the same time they start the IV? That way, you'll just get stuck once."

Mr. Allen allowed that would be a damn sight better plan. Now, if Annie could just sweet-talk somebody over in the main pre-op room to do this. Mouthing another prayer, she got Jan, one of the nicer nurses, on the phone who couldn't have been more understanding.

"Just send him over like he is. I'll start his IV and draw the blood STAT."

"Thanks, Jan, I owe you one."

"Yep, you sure do! Don't worry, I'll collect."

Just then the transportation clerk showed up to collect Mr. Allen.

Suddenly he began talking. "You know, Annie, I tried to tell that dialysis nurse yesterday she wasn't doing it right and she wouldn't listen. So now here I am, having to go through this again. I live with this stuff. I know a few things."

"Mr. Allen, I'm sorry."

"That's all right. It's not your fault, Annie," he actually reached his good arm out a little towards her, almost a wave of sorts.

"We'll see you back here in progressive recovery after surgery, and you'll go home from here. I'll check on you, okay?"

"Yeah, thanks."

And with that, he was on his way. Annie knew there would really be a time crunch to get everything ready on schedule but this patient had earned the right to have some leeway.

Not everyone agreed. Within ten minutes the phone was ringing and it was Annie's favorite psychotic supervisor, Nita.

"Who got Mr. Allen ready this morning?"

"I did, Nita. He has been through a rough time so he didn't have everything..."

Nita couldn't wait for an explanation. "This is totally unacceptable, to send a patient over to us not changed out of his clothes and no blood work done. He isn't going to be ready on time, so maybe you would like to tell Dr. Alfonse why."

"Well, I will talk to him if you want. I had called Jan and we were working together on the situation."

"Once again, you decide which hospital policies you want to follow and which you don't."

"There is a little more to the story than me not following policy."

"I'm sure if you called Janet she would understand and approve of everything, but I am the supervisor over here today so you go by what I say."

Annie then realized that Nita was not interested in any explanation of her actions. Silence, maybe groveling, or possibly self-flagellation with a rubber tourniquet would probably be what Nita would appreciate the most.

Swallow hard.

"I'm sorry things seem so undone but I was trying to . . ."

"Well, sorry isn't good enough, Anna, but that seems to be your way of dealing with your screw-ups. You might try following the rules. They are there for a reason. I am very upset with the quality of this patient's care."

I actually felt pretty good about it.

"I may fill out an incident report on this. I haven't decided yet."

Click.

Part of Annie was actually relieved when Nita chose to abruptly end the conversation, though she had just badly violated telephone etiquette policy. Pausing for a moment with the dead phone receiver in her hand, she reflected on Nita and realized three things: 1. Nita hated her, 2. it was a permanent, irrevocable hatred, 3. though totally illogical, this bothered her intensely and to her core.

To deal with emotional discomfort such as this, Annie had a two-step treatment regimen. Step number one was the Dove Dark Chocolate Bar treatment. Step two was only taken if the first was ineffective. It involved talking to Ben about it when she got home. The good thing about step two was that Ben loved her and was a good listener. The bad thing was, he always had a SOLUTION which usually involved Annie doing something she didn't want to do or which she knew wouldn't work. This forced her to invoke the NO SOLUTIONS – JUST SUPPORT rule. Finally he would put his arms around her, hug her, and tell her what a wonderful person she was. Being reminded of his love helped to negate the bad hateful Nita feelings that had settled on the couch in the living room of her brain, an unwelcome neighbor who wouldn't go home.

Mr. Allen didn't return to progressive recovery until the early afternoon. Although Annie was in pre-op, as soon as she saw him sitting in the recliner she went over to him. It had been so long, she thought it must have been difficult even for a good surgeon like Dr. Alfonse to find a spot to put a new catheter in. Mr. Allen appeared to be sleeping but when Annie approached his side, he opened his eyes.

"There you are, Annie. I made it back!"

"I never had any doubts you would, Mr. Allen. You are too spunky not to."

"Too damn mean is what you really think."

"No, Mr. Allen, I don't. You have dealt with a lot with your illness. It's okay if you don't wear a smile every time you come to the hospital."

"I could hear that nurse fussing at you on the phone for not making me change clothes. I'm sorry you got in trouble on account of an old bastard like me, Annie."

"Hey, Mr. Allen, my day was boring until I checked you in. That lady just likes to yell sometimes. Don't even think a thing about it." How sad that Mr. Allen, with all he had to deal with, had to hear Nita's tirade.

"Anyway, thanks for taking care of me. You are special, Annie, and I don't hand out compliments very often!"

"You know, Mr. Allen, I believe you. You just made my day." A few tears formed, in spite of Annie's best efforts.

"Now, dammit, don't start crying. I can't stand that, you got me? Think you could wrap one of those warm blankets around me without hurting me this time?"

"I'll give it my best shot!" They shared a little smile.

As Annie went to get the blanket, she decided maybe she wouldn't have to eat the Dove bar after all.

■ ■ ■

Christine got so irritated at Annie sometimes. Especially when she cried over nothing. Like that old grouch, Mr. Allen deciding not to cuss at her. That really wasn't something that merited tears. Annie was a nice enough person, but if it weren't for Christine picking up all the loose ends she left undone, Annie wouldn't make it. She never realized that, though. Never really said "thank you" when Christine found important details missing and tried to help Annie correct them. A lot of times people just did not appreciate what you did for them though, that's for sure. It seemed like Christine spent all day at the hospital fixing things and then went home and started all over again. Just last night when she got home late Enos, her husband, was sitting watching TV when she walked in the door. "You know you have a husband who needs you, not just the hospital. There is no supper and I am starving."

"I've got it planned out, I just need a few minutes to get it ready."

"I thought you were supposed to be home at 5:00 today."

"There were late patients, Enos. I couldn't just walk off and leave them."

"No, you could just be late coming home and not have any supper for me."

There was no use trying to explain to Enos. He didn't understand, for one thing; and for another, he wasn't interested. He had a lot of good things about him, but he never had understood the demands of Christine's job. So she tried to remember the good things about Enos, and not look at the not-so-good things. After some concerted effort, she finally thought of something. He always kept the car running well, and never let an inspection sticker expire. Not much at first glance, but Christine was used to working with very little where Enos was concerned. A lot of husbands didn't even care about their wife's cars. She heard them complaining all the time at work. As she cooked up the chicken-fried steak fingers, battered just the way he liked them, she tried to think of the other good things about Enos. He was faithful; he had never strayed. Not that she knew of. But she would have known. He would have left some detail undone and she would have discovered it. If there was one area she excelled in, it was details. She never had discovered anything; therefore, her confidence in her husband's fidelity. As luck would have it, she was right about Enos being faithful. Unfortunately, it was not due to any great devotion to Christine. His job at the plant left him too plain tired to do any fooling around. Then there were the twins, Ed and Ned. They didn't really appreciate her either. At twenty-five, they still hadn't quite found what they wanted to do and consequently did nothing a lot of the time. But they were good boys, they just needed some more growing up time.

She had eighteen steak fingers fried and set to drain and keep warm in the oven in a short time and started mashing the potatoes. Thank goodness, she had gotten up early this morning and boiled them. The men folk would really have a fit if they had to wait for potatoes to boil. Meat and potatoes – that's what her men wanted.

Her feet ached and she looked longingly at the couch, where one of the twins was stretched out.

■ ■ ■

When Annie got home that day, she felt drained physically and emotionally. Ben had gotten home a few minutes earlier, she guessed. He hadn't changed yet but was in the kitchen, putting away the clean dishes from the dishwasher.

"Hey, Hon, you're late. Everything okay?"

"Not really, but it's better now that I'm out of the jaws of the monster (her not-so-affectionate nickname for the hospital)." This claiming of Annie's life had begun with rigid indoctrination in nursing school. There, loyalty to the calling of caring for your patients was instilled with an almost religious intensity. The hospital was made up of other nurses who had been taught in this same vein. So when the nursing manager called on her day off and said, " Two people have called in sick. Can you come in and help out?' it was asked with the expectation that any nurse who had a conscience at all would come. About ninety-nine percent of the time, Annie came. The one percent of the time she didn't, she walked a twisted pathway of agony. First, instead of just saying, "I'm sorry, I can't help out this time", like a normal person would, she felt compelled to give a long and truthful explanation. "I have a doctor's appointment today to get my pap smear." Of course, she was dealing with another nurse who knew the high "guilt factor" of nursing.

"What time is your appointment, could you come in afterwards?"

Even if Annie had planned something else afterwards, if it didn't sound important enough she would usually cave in. If she still managed to resist at this point, the final request would be made, raising the "guilt factor" to critical levels.

"I wouldn't ask you, but there is NO ONE ELSE."

That always left Annie picturing patients lying in beds, begging for water or pain medicine, calling out to an empty hallway. What kind of a person would not respond to this plea? Annie didn't know; she just knew she wasn't one of them.

Ben, even with his job as a physical therapist in a rehab clinic, did not have the same monster issue. Though he cared, he was more detached and, if Annie were completely objective, more normal. He would try to point out to Annie that she was being manipulated. Even though she could see that, she still couldn't say no, just in case there really was an empty hallway and needy patients.

After her quick greeting to Ben, Annie headed straight to the bathroom to take a five-minute shower; an obsessive-compulsive need to "wash the hospital off". She came back quickly to the kitchen and they began working, side-by-side, preparing supper in pleasant silence together. Ben was chopping vegetables for the salad, dicing even squares of the tomatoes with engineer-like precision. Annie began sautéing the chicken breasts in olive oil. She didn't like Ben to cook the chicken. He always overcooked it in an effort to kill any lurking salmonella bugs. However, no living organism could have survived Ben's cooking practices. If the tiniest bit of juice was visible when he mashed the chicken slightly, this was an indication to cook it a good thirty minutes longer. When it had the liquid content equivalent to a slab of cotton, he would pronounce it done.

"Tell me about your day," Ben offered her the floor.

"You wouldn't believe it; I had another run-in with that nurse manager, Nita." Annie carefully related the story of Mr. Allen and how she had tried to intervene for him. As she told about the vicious conversation with Nita, Ben interrupted her.

"I told you that you should have reported her the first time she was so ugly to you. You've got to report her this time, she is threatening you. That's wrong."

I knew he would say this.

"Ben, I love you, but I don't want any solutions, I just want you to listen and support me."

They had been through versions of this same conversation so many times over the years that Ben knew immediately what to do. He stopped chopping tiny identically sized squares of carrots and put his arms around her, as she stood at the stove.

"Okay, but you can't blame me for trying. I do love you, Annie. I just don't like to see you get hurt."

"Thanks, Ben, I love you too. The chicken is done."

"Did you check to make sure it's not pink inside?"

Sigh.

5

MEMORANDUM

STATUS: PRIORITY HIGH
SUBJECT: CPR POLICY AND PROCEDURE REVIEW
TO: NURSE MANAGERS OF ALL UNITS
FROM: RISK MANAGEMENT
THERE IS AN URGENT NEED FOR REVIEW OF CPR POLICY AND PROCEDURE FOR ALL YOUR NURSING STAFF. PLEASE SCHEDULE STAFF INSERVICE REVIEW THIS WEEK, MANDATORY FOR ALL STAFF. THE STAFF RN IS NOT AUTHORIZED TO PRONOUNCE PATIENT DEAD, ONLY MD CAN MAKE THIS DECISION. THE ONLY EXCEPTION IS THE 11 TO 7 NURSING SUPERVI-SOR WHEN HOUSE DOCTOR IS UNAVAILABLE.

The next morning, who was on the surgery schedule but Mrs. Olmos. The lymph node biopsy had come back positive. This time she was scheduled to get a special catheter inserted into her veins so she could receive chemotherapy. As usual, the large Olmos clan was gathered together in the waiting room as Annie went out to get the patient.

Annie heard the now familiar greeting, "There my nurse, come here." As she walked over to her, she noticed that her patient's pallor. "Hi, Mrs. Olmos, how are you?"

"Oh, so-so, Annie, how are you? You take care of me today, okay?"

"Sure, Mrs. Olmos, be glad to. I'll make sure the big room is available. Be right back and get you!"

As she went back to pre-op to see if the large room six was empty, Christine called out from another room. "I saved room six for Mrs. Olmos."

Because it was so rare, it was always touching to Annie when Christine revealed the big soft spot in her heart.

"Thanks, Chris! She really needs her family with her, even though there's a lot of them."

No answer.

The fatigue infused the room like a heavy fog, covering the entire Olmos family. The constant concern they felt for the matriarch was taking a toll on all of them. Mr. Olmos, a quiet man anyway, seemed to fade away into a corner of the room and Annie noticed the shadows under his eyes. Even the grandchildren were subdued this morning. The seriousness of Mrs. Olmos' illness was becoming evident to all. She was going to be admitted to a hospital room after her procedure today. If all went well, she would start her first chemotherapy treatment tomorrow.

"Annie, you come check on me in the hospital, okay?"

"Sure, I'll come by tomorrow. You already have plenty of nurses, though. You don't really need me," Annie gestured around at the well-filled room.

"No, Annie, I need you," was her quick response. "You like Mexican food, Annie?"

"I can't think of one kind of Mexican food I don't like, except tripas."

Mrs. Olmos chucked, "You know what tripas is?"

"I'm not sure exactly what part of the cow it is, Mrs. O, I just know I don't like it."

"For some reason, it seemed funny to the whole family that Annie didn't like tripas.

"You like tamales, Annie, I make you my special tamales."

Home-made tamales were like nothing else. The masa coating in home-made tamales was soft and chewy, while restaurant tamales could be tough and leathery. The filling in home-made tamales was tasty and spicy, and not dripping with grease, like a restaurant tamale. Annie had never made tamales, but she had heard stories from some of her Hispanic friends that tamales were one of the most labor-intensive foods to make, taking up to three days. Annie really didn't want Mrs. Olmos to go to that kind of trouble but she didn't know what to say.

"I know whatever kind of food you make is good, Mrs. Olmos, but aren't tamales a lot of work?"

"All my daughters came over last weekend and we made tamales. They in the freezer. I bring you some."

"That would really be a treat. Thanks, Mrs. Olmos."

After finishing the food discussion, Annie suddenly felt the aching emptiness of her stomach, and a tamale/cup of coffee breakfast break sounded mighty good about now. But breakfast breaks were a rare event; indeed, they occurred with the frequency of a lunar eclipse.

Mrs. Olmos' procedure went smoothly and Annie checked on her in recovery just to say a quick hello. As Annie walked away, she couldn't help but think how surprising it was that she had become friends with this particular patient.

■ ■ ■

The next morning was unusually dark, a heavy fog having settled over the area like a soft, white blanket. Annie had to borrow Ben's car that morning, due to the fact her car wouldn't start. He was very particular about his car and although Annie had never been in an accident, he seemed to have a fear she would choose the time to do so while driving his car.

"Park at the back of the lot, where you won't get scratched by any other cars."

"Ben, I will be careful. I have never scratched your car, for heaven's sake."

"But if you park where it's crowded, other people could pull up too close and scratch it."

He continued on, in driving instructor mode, "and drive slowly in this fog, and don't use your bright beams, they just cut down on your visibility."

This was beginning to get irritating and Annie, not too calmly, reminded Ben she had been driving for over twenty years, even in fog occasionally, and was accident-free. By the time, she pulled out of the driveway, her confidence was a little shaken.

"What if I actually do have an accident this day of all days?" As a result of the early morning instructions and the fears they instilled, she drove at a snail's pace. A long line of cars quickly accumulated behind her, unable to pass because of the low visibility.

The dark hospital parking lot looked virtually deserted. The lights were so muted by the fog that the hospital itself was barely visible from the back row where Annie had carefully maneuvered the car. Last row, in the corner, as instructed by Ben.

There was one other car parked on the same row, but she had avoided even the hint of being close to another vehicle. As she got out of the car, she glanced towards the other car, just to be sure there was not a serial murderer making his way stealthily towards her. This fog made her feel so alone and she shivered as she remembered a chapter in the mystery she had been reading last night, *One Fine Foggy Day*. There may have been other people closer in, but they were invisible to Annie.

"No serial murderer sighted. So far, so good," she said out loud in an effort to laugh at her fears.

As she started to walk away, she noticed that someone had left a big trash bag or something beside the other car. As she peered for a closer look, it seemed to be a jacket, and there were some shoes, too. Wait, no, that couldn't be . . . as she walked closer she saw that, indeed, it was a body.

She ran over the rest of the way and stooped down. It was pitch dark out here but she could see it was a man. She reached down and felt for his carotid pulse, locating the spot by rote. His skin was ice-cold and there was no pulse. He had been dead for more than just a few minutes, of that much she was certain. There was no point in trying resuscitation, it would have been pointless. What if he had been murdered? She knew one of the key rules was: Don't touch anything at the scene, don't move anything, don't disturb anything. Calling out, "Help me, somebody!" she peered intently into the maddening fog but out here in the back row at 5:30 in the morning there was no one. She didn't want to leave the body. It just didn't seem right. Finally her mind started functioning again and she remembered her cell phone. She fumbled in her purse, finally locating it at the very bottom, of course. Dialing 911 never took so long.

After Annie calmly relayed the sketchy information she had to the 911 operator, she noticed that she was shaking all over.

The operator, in an effort to keep Annie talking, seemed to be asking random stupid questions.

"Are you sure the man is dead? "

"Yes."

"Can you check his pupils with a flashlight to see if there is a reaction?"

"No." Annie noticed her mind was having trouble making a coherent string of words into a simple sentence. She couldn't seem to tell the 911operator that she didn't have a flashlight, and it was too dark to even see the man's features, much less check his pupils.

Soon she heard the faint sound of a siren and was relieved not to be alone with only the 911 operator and the stupid questions. Suddenly realizing a hospital supervisor should be notified, she hung up and called the hospital. It was a relief to be talking to the hospital operator instead of Mrs. Question Lady from 911.

But first, Annie had to convince her to contact the supervisor about a body in the parking lot. This did not seem to fit any of the prescribed emergencies listed on the operator's critical action sheet. After what seemed forever, the operator connected Annie to the acting nurse supervisor. The ring tones on the phone calmed Annie just a little, reminding her help would be here soon.

"What is going on in the parking lot? Who am I speaking too?"

Oh, no.

"Nita, this is Annie, and the police are almost here. I wanted you to know what's going on."

"Yes, I think that would be a good idea. Where are the police, why are they coming here, and who called them?"

"I did. I am in the back parking lot on the back corner. There is a body back here."

"What do you mean, a body?"

"A dead person, Nita, someone who is not alive anymore, that's what it usually means!" Annie's stress level was fast approaching critical mass and she tended towards sarcasm under stress.

"Don't you disrespect me . . . "

"The police are here, Nita, I have to go."

"Don't say anything, this could be a legal risk for the hospital. I am coming right now. I'll answer any questions, understand me? Which parking lot are you in, the South or East?"

This question of directions momentarily stumped Annie. She suffered from directional dyslexia and had no map in her brain with north/south/ east/west. As a result, there was an unusually long pause, which aggravated Nita further.

"You better tell me where you are right now, Anna."

"Uh, it's the one that faces the day surgery, whichever one that is."

There was no way Annie could simply stand mute as the police arrived. She tried to explain how she had discovered the body but began to feel slightly nauseated. This symptom meant she was going to faint. One of the policemen led her to the front of the car, away from the body, so she could sit and put her head down a moment. Nita arrived breathlessly on the scene. Annie heard her and inwardly groaned.

"I am the nursing supervisor. I will answer any questions from now on." Nita came towards the front of the car where Annie sat on the hard concrete.

"Go on in to your unit. I'll talk to you later. I will handle things from here. You didn't say anything, did you?'

"I just told them how I found him and that he was already cold and without a pulse."

"Anna, I told you not to answer any questions. You did attempt CPR, I'm sure, but why did you stop, because the police got here?

"No, I didn't do CPR. This man was dead, there was no point . . ."

"That is not for you to decide. You always do CPR. A physician needs to be the one to tell you to stop. You know that. What were you thinking? This could be a hospital legal nightmare. Did you ever stop to consider that? No, you were busy making medical decisions you had no business making. This is a Code 13 situation, and you have only made it worse. What were you thinking?"

Annie was too nauseated and shaky to answer, so she remained mute, which happened to be Nita's favorite condition for her. With a flick of her clipboard, she wordlessly dismissed Annie, walking back towards the policemen.

Annie thought it must be wonderful to be so full of confidence about handling any situation without hesitation. And as far as Annie could tell, Nita never seemed to be plagued with any doubts about the correctness of her decisions. The ambulance was pulling up as Annie shakily made her way to Day Surgery.

The fog remained thick and unrelenting, but from the windows of the Day Surgery unit, the flashing lights of the ambulance and police car could just be made out. Everyone, it appeared – patients and nurses together – were standing peering out the windows that faced the south parking lot, trying to figure out what was going on. As Annie walked into pre-op, she saw Christine sitting at the desk busily working on charts, the only one actually on duty.

When Christine looked up and saw her, she immediately got up and came over to her. "What is the matter with you? You look really pale. Come in here and sit down." Chris quickly went into nurse mode, got Annie into a recliner in a patient room, put a cold washcloth on her head, and lay the recliner back. Then she put one of those nice warm blankets over Annie. It really did feel comforting, just like patients said.

"Thanks, Chris, I'll be OK in a minute. I was just a little faint feeling, but it's already getting better. Did anyone ever tell you that you're a good nurse?" Annie managed a weak smile to her friend.

"Not too often – thank you! What's going on with you?"

Sipping on a cold Coke that Chris had provided from Patient Supply, no less, Annie gradually related what had happened. Chris listened and then quietly said, "You should have tried CPR, Annie, even though you knew he was dead."

"To me that would have been disrespectful to a dead person's body. I just couldn't do that to someone. It was so obvious he was gone."

"Well, I hope you don't get into trouble, that's all," was Chris's only response. Not too reassuring, but Annie couldn't believe there would be any trouble. Of course, Nita had said this was a Code 13 – hospital terminology for an "unexpected occurrence" that occurred on hospital property. The unspoken possibility of every Code 13 was a lawsuit, an event to be dreaded even more than death itself in the eyes of the hospital administration.

By this time of the morning, although it remained as dark as night outside, not all the first patients of the day were checked in and ready and it seemed everyone realized it at once. Within minutes nurses walked away from the window and the normal buzz of activity in pre-op began. Annie felt recovered from her weak spell and transformed from being a patient to being a nurse again.

During the morning, word gradually filtered around of Annie's parking lot experience. Her co-workers seemed pretty evenly divided over how she had handled it. But Annie knew in her heart she had done nothing wrong. Nothing would have brought that poor man back.

About eight that morning Janet called Annie in pre-op. "Annie, can you come to my office for a few minutes right now? Nita is here and needs to talk to you."

"Sure, Janet, give me five minutes to report off to somebody about my patients and I'll be there."

"OK, Annie. No longer, please."

Annie walked through the hallway towards Janet's office with a queasy flutter in her stomach and she noticed her feet felt numb and leaden, making it hard to walk at a brisk pace. As she opened the door Janet and Nita were sitting at the desk, no sounds of conversation. Thick air sat in the room, which seemed gray as if the fog from outside had filtered in through the vents, though the overhead lights shone brightly. Janet's desk was filled with several piles of papers of differing heights, and post-it notes were perched around the phone base like yellow confetti. There wasn't a chair available for Annie in this compact space, which was part of a conversion from a conference room to three tiny offices. As the door closed, Nita seemed to become bigger, her anger filling the room and mashing on Annie, a rough push on her chest. Nita had her clipboard fully loaded with papers and her mouth was a tiny little line.

"Nita's been telling me about the Code 13 in the parking lot this morning. You should have told me immediately, Annie."

"I'm sorry. I meant to. I got busy checking in patients because I was running behind and I just forgot."

"See what I mean, Janet? How can someone forget about a dead body in the parking lot? I don't see how you deal with her."

"I didn't forget about the death, I mean I was just real busy with getting patients ready and it slipped my mind to call you, Janet. You know how crazy pre-op gets in the mornings."

Janet solemnly said, "Nita needs to get some information about the situation. Just answer her questions, you and I will talk later." Annie recognized that soft, flat tone and knew she had let Janet down. She so wished she could replay this morning, and re-make the beginning of what seemed to be a very bad movie. If only her car had started, none of this would have happened. She wouldn't have taken Ben's car, wouldn't have parked on the back row, wouldn't have stumbled on the body. Some other nurse, one who would follow hospital policy, would have found the body. Right now Nita would be taking that nurse out for coffee and congratulating her. Nita cleared her throat loudly and jarred Annie back to the present.

Annie started relating how she had discovered the body, and her actions that followed. Though she tried to avoid eye contact, in this small space, it was a challenge. There was nowhere to look but the floor, and that seemed to add to her feelings of guilt.

"So, Anna, what was the reason you decided to not follow hospital policy and start CPR on this individual?"

"Well, his skin was quite cold and it was obvious he had been dead a while and doing CPR would have not only been useless, it would have been wrong in my opinion."

"You are not in a position to re-write hospital policy in a parking lot, Anna. There is a reason that we have policy, and it is to be followed. It's not just a list of helpful suggestions."

"There was another reason I didn't want to touch him. I thought maybe he had been murdered and in that case, it would be wrong to disturb a crime scene."

"Whatever gave you the idea he was murdered? That is completely ridiculous," Nita interjected and Annie wondered if maybe she really had read too many murder mysteries. It did sound kind of far out, she realized just a tad too late after the words had left her mouth and lay in the air like the ravings of a delusional person.

"Well, a big part of the problem, Nita, is that it was pitch black. Because of the fog I could hardly see him, much less try to decide what had happened to him. I was just trying to consider all possibilities very quickly. Sorry that you think my ideas were ridiculous. I'm not as smart as you, I guess."

"You certainly won't get any argument from me on that point, Anna. The problem as I see it, you didn't just make one mistake, you made several. And they are pretty big ones, I might add. I am on my way to administration to make a complete report. I'll be back with you later on today, to let you know what the administration committee says. Furthermore, Anna, you are to talk to no one about this until we have made some decisions, am I understood?"

"Nita, most of the people up here know that I found a body in the parking lot. It's not something that I would leave out of my conversation. Plus everyone could see the ambulance and police car."

"That is just great. Well, make it confidential from now on. No more talk about it at all."

" Can I ask you one more thing, though?"

Nita didn't answer, but with her best murderous expression, and small sparks seeming to flash from her eyes, she simply looked at Annie as if daring her to actually ask. But Annie felt such a curiosity, she pressed on.

"Do you know who the man was?"

"That information is on a "need to know" basis for now, Anna."

"I found him. Don't I have a right to know who he was?"

"I'm sure word will leak out soon enough, but I am not here to answer YOUR questions. I'm here for you to answer MY questions."

The stream of anger was taking a toll and Annie felt tears coming. She did not want Nita to get the enjoyment of witnessing them.

"Do you have any more questions, Nita? It really is a busy day, and someone is covering my patients, but I didn't think this would be a long meeting. I need to let them know if I'm not coming back soon."

Janet quietly verified to Nita how heavy the schedule was today, which suddenly made it believable to her.

"You are free to go for now, Anna. DO NOT talk about this at all to anyone, under any circumstance. Understood?" Annie just nodded her head and made a quick exit.

There was absolutely no private area in Day Surgery where one could "come apart" in solitude. The closest thing to private Annie could think of was the stairwell and she almost ran to get there. Breathing in and out deeply, she first gave herself her "I didn't do anything wrong" lecture and followed that with her "nothing bad is going to happen" pep talk. The denial mode that she depended on so much just wasn't working very well this morning and did nothing to stop her tears. She hated going to take care of patients with her eyes all red, evidence of her "come apart." After going to the restroom and putting cold paper towels on her eyes then looking in the mirror, she felt even worse. When Annie cried, it showed. She envied people who could cry a few minutes, then dab gently at the corners of their eyes and look fine. Her eyelids, on the other hand, had already swollen to twice their size. Her nose had begun a steady stream. This required repeated wiping, which left it redder and noticeably larger. In fact, the longer she looked at it the larger it seemed to be.

As she stood staring at her drippy image in the mirror, she heard some muffled words coming from somewhere nearby. She couldn't decipher them but there was a desperate, angry tone to them. She exited the restroom and immediately saw the origin of the noise. The nearby door to the men's restroom was partly open and protruding was part of a wheelchair. A suspiciously familiar pair of dirty khaki pants was visible. The wheelchair rider had gotten jammed in the doorway. Calling for help was interspersed with long phrases of profanity directed at the "damn stupid ignorant door." Annie was certain she knew the identity of the person, so she called out, "Mr. Allen, is that you?"

"Just get me out, now. The damn wheel is stuck."

Together, she pulled as he pushed and after a few tries, the obstruction was freed and he was through the door.

"You were in kind of a jam there, weren't you, Mr. Allen? I'm glad I happened to be close by. Are you okay now?"

"Oh, it's you, Annie, is it? No, I'm not okay. How would you like to be trapped and not able to get out and it's not your fault?"

I think I know how you feel. "I don't think I'd like it very much, either. Do you need me to take you somewhere?"

He paused and seemed to hesitate. Annie noticed a crumpled piece of paper protruding from his pocket.

"Would that paper help us know where to go?" She gently removed it and read out the appointment time and office number.

"Hell, yes, that's it. Just took me a minute. Gimme that paper back."

Trying to cover for his momentary confusion, she said in her perkiest nurse voice, "Sure, no problem. Let's head for the elevator." Annie grabbed the wheelchair handles and began to briskly roll Mr. Allen along, knowing she was already missing in action in Day Surgery and needing to get forward progress started.

"Hey, what the hell are you doing? I'm not totally helpless yet, you know."

"I'm sorry, Mr. Allen, I didn't realize you wanted to wheel yourself. I should have asked you."

So the progression to the elevator, which had begun at a brisk pace, decelerated considerably. Mr. Allen's one speed was SLOW. As the wheelchair squeaked along, Annie started feeling like she wanted to scream.

After a pace which turtles could have zipped past, they arrived at the elevator. Of course the first time the door opened, it was already filled to capacity. But finally the elevator, which seemed to have the same traveling speed as Mr. Allen, opened and there was room for them to enter. When they arrived at number 414, Annie was glad she was there because Mr. Allen needed someone to hold the door open for him.

"Well, bye for now Mr. Allen. Take care."

He was already wheeling up to the check-in desk, intent on signing in. *Thanks for all your help. No, no, don't mention it.*

People often didn't mean to be rude; they were just so wrapped up in their illnesses they didn't think outside of themselves, Annie had to remind herself.

Walking back into pre-op, she found Teresa.

"Baby, what is the matter? Darlin', are you alright?"

She realized that her red eyes and nose had not had time to clear yet. "Yeah, Teresa, I'll be fine in a minute, thanks. If I just focus on work, it will help. I am not supposed to talk about anything, I'm sorry."

"That Nita, she can be so mean. Don't you worry, baby, everything's going to work out."

For some reason, those words – really just a meaningless platitude – helped Annie's denial mode kick back in.

"You know, you're probably right, Teresa. I know I didn't do anything wrong."

"There you go, girl." Teresa followed that word with a rib-cracking hug and Annie felt all better now, thank you very much.

By lunchtime, things had slowed a bit but were due to get busy again in the afternoon.

"Chris, I think I'll run over and check on Mrs. Olmos. I promised her I would visit her in her hospital room. I'll just use that as my lunch break."

"Fine, Annie, tell her the nurse that asks too many questions says, 'Hi'."

Locating the patient room number in the computer, Annie walked briskly over the walkway to the hospital. When she got to the room, two of Mrs. Olmos' daughters were standing outside the room crying.

There must be some bad news. Maybe Mrs. Olmos had a complication. Annie stopped briefly where they stood.

"Hi."

"Oh, Annie, I'm glad you're here, you know." One daughter spoke up, but then continued sobbing.

"I'm sorry." Annie really didn't know what else to say. The daughters were both obviously overcome with sadness now. "Should I come back another time?"

"No, no, she needs you, go in . . . maybe you can help her, she is so upset. When you love someone so much, you . . ."

Annie could see how overwhelmed both the daughters were. It did help sometimes to have an objective person who could be more supportive and less emotional.

She tapped on the door lightly and then gently pushed it open. The room was dark and the usually chatty TV sat silent and gray. Mrs. Olmos, lying curled up in a fetal position in bed, had her back to the door but Annie could hear her sobs.

"Mrs. Olmos, it's me, Annie. I wanted to check on you. Is it okay if I come in?"

Mrs. Olmos didn't answer but waved her arm, motioning Annie to come close. Annie approached the bed. Mrs. Olmos took hold of her hand, squeezing it to the point of pain. Annie sensed that she should just be there, not say or do anything. Maybe the cancer had shown signs of further spread, or maybe she couldn't take the chemo. Whatever it was, she was more distraught than Annie had ever seen her.

What she said next did not make sense.

"Mi querido, he was so good to me. Why?" Then she was overcome with weeping again.

"What's happened, Mrs. Olmos?"

"Oh, Annie, mi esposo, my husband, is gone.

"Oh, Mrs. Olmos, I'm so very sorry. What happened?"

"He was coming in early to stay with me before he had to work. He work so hard."

Annie remembered the very first time she had met Mrs. Olmos. Mr. Olmos, and how hard he worked, had been one of the first things she had talked about.

"Somebody found him in the parking lot. They didn't even try to help him and he died."

Annie inhaled a muffled cry. She swayed a little and held onto the side rails of the bed. It was him! Quiet, kind Mr. Olmos --Annie could picture him loading up the fajitas and beans to send home with her not very long ago. Now this little woman with all she was facing, along with her loyal clan had suffered a horrendous blow.

"Mrs. Olmos, what do you mean, nobody helped him?"

"I hear one of the nurses say the nurse that found him didn't even try to "susitate" him, just walked away. That make me so angry. Why she not even try to help him? Treating him like a dead dog . . ."

Part of Annie wanted to cry out, "No, no, that's not how it happened at all." But mostly, Annie wanted to: 1. Not be in this room, 2. With this lady, 3. At this moment in time. Abruptly explaining that she was on her lunch break, she pulled her hand back, trying to free herself from Mrs. Olmos' strong grip. As her patient released her, she reached up and patted Annie's face, gently dismissing her without another word.

Annie left the room at a brisk pace, almost colliding with Nita in the hallway.

"What are you doing here, Anna? You should not be here, under any circumstance."

The two daughters, who were still standing outside the door, misunderstood the situation. "Oh, that's okay, Miss, Annie is my mother's favorite nurse. She wanted to see her."

Mercifully, Nita didn't go into the complicated details with them. "She is supposed to stay on her unit in Day Surgery unless transferring a patient, that's all. I need to speak with her privately, I'm sure you understand. I'll be back to check on your mother in a few minutes." She gave the daughters an odd little expression, which was Nita's attempt at a smile. Since she used the smile muscles so infrequently, it came out looking more like a grimace and was weirdly disconcerting. Nita nodded towards Annie to follow her.

Annie wondered what could possibly go wrong next. She was pretty sure Nita would never believe she didn't know about the identity of the body. Being right, in this case, was not much consolation.

"You have a lot of nerve, Anna, I'll give you that much. To think you could just waltz over here and see this patient, of all the patients in the hospital. I could terminate you here on the spot. This is gross misconduct in a Code 13 situation. God only knows what you said in there. I will meet you in Day Surgery in Janet's office in fifteen minutes. Tell her I need her there as a witness. Do not go back on the Day Surgery unit. You are not to have contact with any patient – none at all!"

Annie, knowing that it would do no good, still had to speak. "Nita, I know this may be hard to believe, but I didn't know Mr. Olmos was the man I found until a few minutes ago when Mrs. Olmos told me."

"You are right about one thing, it is hard to believe. In fact, I would go so far as to say it is impossible to believe. Of course, maybe Janet will believe you. You have managed to convince her of other unbelievable things. Anything else come to mind you'd like to try out on me?"

Annie wished so badly for a stinging retort, but sadly none came. The stinging retort part of her brain seemed to have failed her.

"No."

"I'll see you shortly." Exit Nita with a flourish of her clipboard, and what almost looked like the beginnings of real smile on her face.

Annie slowly made her way down the hallways back to Day Surgery. Her mind felt numb, thoughts sitting still like water in a stopped-up sink. She found Janet on the unit and relayed Nita's message.

"Annie, I haven't talked with her or with administration yet, but this may be serious. I just want to prepare you."

"I'm starting to get that feeling."

Then Annie had to tell Janet how she had visited Mrs. Olmos and there discovered the identity of the dead man. Thank God, Janet believed her. Before they talked further, Nita met them in the hallway outside of Janet's office.

"Shall we go in?"

If Annie hadn't known better, it would have sounded like an invitation from Nita to a grand event. Maybe to Nita it was.

"This will be brief and to-the-point. Anna, you are in serious breach of following prescribed hospital policy, resulting in a Code 13. You are being placed on administrative leave, effective immediately. You are to leave the hospital property now and you will not return until instructed to do so. A formal investigation of your actions will probably take three to five days. You are not to talk to anyone about what you did, or more accurately what you didn't do."

As Annie looked at Nita, she realized that she had been right about at least one of her observations. That had been a little smile on Nita's face she had seen. It seemed to be all Nita could do to keep from bursting into song at this point. Annie's mind was still functioning in the "stopped up sink" mode, and she didn't trust herself to speak. Because of this, she was as surprised as anyone by what she said next as there seemed to be no functioning connection between her brain and her mouth; she spoke with all the emotion of an aging robot.

"I didn't do anything wrong."

Of course, this assessment of the situation was not very impressive to anyone in the room, especially Nita.

"I am not interested in your opinion of your actions, Anna. You will have a time to speak to the investigation committee when they have completed their work." Nita picked up the phone and asked the operator to page security.

Janet spoke for the first time. "Nita, what are you doing?"

"It is standard procedure for security to escort any suspended employee off of hospital premises, no exceptions."

Her smile was quite evident now, even to Janet. "I don't know why you are smiling, Nita. That is very inappropriate. I'm sure the committee might be interested in why you find it so amusing to suspend a loyal employee and a great nurse. And believe me, I will not hesitate to tell them."

The smile was gone as suddenly as it appeared. A small victory. "Janet, you are part of the management team. I expect your support."

Annie saw Janet's jaw tighten and her voice became very soft, an ominous sign. "I am supporting the investigation. I am not supporting the way you are handling it. This is one of my best nurses and I don't appreciate the way this is being done." Of course Annie knew Janet thought all of her Day Surgery nurses were the best, but it still helped to hear that just at this moment.

This was like pouring hot oil on Nita. She stood up, looked at them both and said, "I am disgusted with both of you. Anna, you are getting what you deserve, nothing less. It's surprising nothing like this has happened to you before, the way you so easily dismiss hospital policy. You expect me to be sad over this. I'm not. Rules are important – the most important thing, in fact. Without rules, bad things can happen; in fact our whole society can collapse. Why can't you understand that?"

Annie was puzzled that the structure of society and the hospital policy were interconnected in any way. For a brief moment their eyes met. Annie saw fear – and a look that reminded her of her eccentric Aunt Maude, who lived with bedsheets covering every window and stuffed along the edges of the doors, " to keep the poisonous gas out." Nita quickly turned away, holding her clipboard next to her heart and looked out the window in silence. The phone call from security broke the quiet.

Nita instructed them to come to Janet's office to escort an employee out. "I'm leaving now. You are to wait here. Janet, will you please stay with her until security gets here?"

"Yes, Nita, I will. Thank you, you can go now."

Nita didn't like the fact that she was being dismissed, but there was not much she could do. She turned and, smile back in place, walked out of the office leaving Annie and Janet both speechless.

Janet reached over and took Annie's hand. " I am so sorry. I don't know what to say. Don't give up, it has to get better after they complete the investigation."

Annie just looked at Janet who was blurry and out of focus because of the tears which had filled her eyes to the overflow level.

"I don't understand. He was dead, Janet. He had been dead for a while."

"Remember, Annie, you aren't supposed to talk about it. They will ask you that, and I want you to be able to answer truthfully."

A knock on the door ended their "illegal" conversation. It was Max from security. "Excuse me, I must have misunderstood Mrs. Stromeyer. Can I use your phone to page her?"

Janet corrected Max. "No, Max, this is the right place. Will you walk Annie out to her car?"

"Annie, gosh, you? I'm sure sorry to have to do this."

"That's okay, Max. It's not your fault. I need to get my purse from my locker first. Janet, call me when you know what I am supposed to do next."

With Janet's assurances and Max's look of concern, she was able to exit without totally collapsing. She was pretty shaky, though, and thankful that she did not run into any of her co-workers in the locker room. This was not a time for explanations, especially when she had none to give.

Annie's mind was going off into all kinds of weird scenarios and she felt like Alice in Wonderland as Alice fell down the hole following the white rabbit. It really was getting "curiouser and curiouser". Now that she thought about it, Nita bore a remarkable resemblance to the Queen of

Hearts. It would not sound at all out of character for her to scream out, "Off with her head, off with her head!"

Max, the quiet security man, was waiting with an anxious expression as she came out of the locker room. Maybe he thought she was going to go berserk and start ripping out lockers. She felt the need to reassure him although ripping out something would feel pretty good about now. "It's okay, Max. I'm okay."

He nervously jingled the large wad of keys hanging at his belt. It seemed to make a little tune, like a child in kindergarten playing in the rhythm band. Annie had to suppress an urge to do a little jig in time to the jingling keys and realized she was close to losing it.

They walked together wordlessly for a while towards the parking lot. It was just too hard to try to make conversation when you were being escorted off your job by security.

"I can make it from here, Max, my car's on the last row. Thanks."

"Miss Annie, I'm sorry, I have to see you get in your car. I'm real sorry, that's just the rules."

Annie was surprised that anything could make her feel any worse, but this did. But she was through making any exceptions to hospital policy, no matter how insane the rule seemed to be.

"Oh, I didn't know the rules. Sorry, Max. I'm the one in trouble."

Together they approached her car. He waited as she unlocked it and got in.

"Hope this all works out for you, Miss Annie."

"Yeah, I hope so too, Max. Thanks."

She rolled the window up noiselessly, not wanting to breathe in any more contaminated air from the EVIL hospital.

Maybe I will die from the heat of this oven-like car. Annie tried to picture a little tear coming from Nita's eyes when she read the news of Annie's passing, (I was too hard on the poor girl and now her blood is on my hands. Oh Annie, I'm sorry) but when she couldn't muster up a vision of even a sad look, much less a tear, on Nita's face she rolled the window down at the first traffic light and turned the air conditioning to high. The cold wind of the AC blowing like a brisk breeze on her face was calming and seemed to reorient her. She glanced down at the speedometer and realized she was going 50 miles per hour in what was a 30 mile per hour zone. Pulling her foot back from the gas pedal and taking a deep breath, she began to sort through her thoughts. Annie quickly found this to be a daunting task, like trying to match socks with the lights out. All that she could focus on was getting home.

Remembering long car trips as a child going from Texas to California to see Grandma and the familiar question, "are we there yet?" she felt that same impatience now. The fifteen minute trip seemed suspended in time and when finally Annie turned into the driveway she was exhausted. Bear, the dog, was waiting at the gate and followed her in softly. Entering the empty house, the quietness felt safe. The pop of the Diet Coke can as she opened it broke the silence briefly. Going to the comfortable chair, she sat down and sipped the Coke as her mind zipped about like a fly looking for a place to land. Annie decided to try not thinking, to see if she could get her mind to calm down. She stared at the brown upholstery of the chair arm just focusing on one spot and did some deep breathing. What went wrong? Why does Nita hate me so much? Did I really do something wrong? Her mind wasn't cooperating.

Well, so much for relaxation techniques.

Suddenly Bear ambled over and unexpectedly jumped up on her lap. She and Ben, on a whim one Saturday about five years ago, had rescued this sweet little black mutt from the pound. Bear must weigh fifty pounds by now and was well beyond being a lap dog, by most standards. Her long legs hung over the chair's edge. But Bear simply curled up, as best she could, and lay there. Her weight and the warmth of her body were comforting to Annie. She stroked the incredible softness of Bear's ears a few times but stopped, unable to give out anything to anybody else right now. But Bear seemed to understand that Annie needed comforting and didn't move from her lap for over an hour. When she did get up, she curled up at Annie's feet and plopped her head on Annie's toes, willing her to stay there.

With the phone and TV controller in reach, Annie had no desire to move. She flicked on the TV and placidly pushed the channel button. Coming to rest on *What Not To Wear*, she learned that with her hips she shouldn't wear tapered jeans.

"They make you look like an ice cream cone," the host of the show told the woman being evaluated who had a body shape remarkably like Annie's. Annie thought that she would cry if someone said that to her on national TV. The woman contestant, however, just stood looking sheepish as if it had been found out she was, indeed, trying to impersonate an ice cream cone.

As that show ended, Annie sat motionless as a program about tattoos came on the screen. Annie became pleasantly lost in watching the subculture of the world of tattoos. People coming in to get permanently labeled in memory of their grandfather, grandmother, or another special person in their lives or to mark a special occasion were especially fascinating, for that tattoo was a glimpse into the heart.

There seemed to be something therapeutic about getting a tattoo. Annie wished she were brave enough to get one. She knew just what it would be – a hummingbird, one of her favorite of God's creatures. She could never see one without smiling. It would have been good today, on this black day, to be able to peek down beside her belly button at a feisty little hummingbird drinking nectar from a beautiful pink hibiscus flower. They didn't seem to realize their size in the giant world they inhabited. One would buzz and dive-bomb another who came too near to the mass of red salvias blooming profusely in her back yard flowerbed.

"As if your little stomach could hold all that nectar," Annie would quietly fuss at the aggressor. "There's plenty here for fifty other hummingbirds. Be nice." But the hummingbird would not be deterred from protecting what he determined was his territory. In a way, she admired his spunkiness, a "pit bull" personality in the tiniest of birds.

In a random channel search, Annie stumbled onto one of her all-time favorite movies, *To Kill a Mockingbird*. It was great to see Atticus Finch fight prejudice and injustice with such grace. This time she felt more connected to Boo Radley, hiding behind the door, afraid of the world.

I never really understood Boo Radley before. This is a bad sign.

Finally, it was time for *Oprah*. It was then Annie realized she had been sitting in the same spot almost since she had gotten home. She watched abused women tell their stories and felt a strange connection to them, too, as life felt simply beyond her control. A big difference was that she had Ben. She was so thankful to know he would be there for her, no matter what. She didn't want to talk to anybody right now, though, and when the phone's ringing interrupted *Oprah*, she put it under a pillow. She wanted to talk to Ben face-to-face. She would just wait, safe in her brown chair with her black dog resting on her toes until Ben was home.

Annie knew that if *Oprah* was over she should have supper planned, or at least started. All the meat in the house was still in the freezer, and it never tasted right when she defrosted it in the microwave. Frying eggs for supper, her emergency standby meal, seemed as overwhelming as a ten course dinner and the thought of actually swallowing food was nauseating to her right now. At last, something positive. *Maybe I will loose weight, along with my mind and my job.*

The sound of a car pulling into the driveway interrupted Annie's thoughts. Still, she didn't move. Bear, who was usually up with tail wagging rhythmically and headed for the back door looked up, but otherwise didn't move either. Both of them seemed to be stuck where they were. As Ben opened the back door, he gave a quick whistle. This was a warning that he was in the house. The habit was a result of him coming home early one day, unbeknownst to Annie who was soaking and dozing in a hot bubble bath, home early also. Ben walked into the bathroom, causing Annie to scream so loudly that the next-door neighbor called the police, thinking a crime was in progress. The whole incident had scared both of them although Annie claimed that being nude at the time, she suffered more mental anguish than Ben. The policeman who came didn't help the situation much. He felt everything could have been prevented if Annie hadn't let out such a blood-curdling scream. As if that were something she had sat in the tub planning out maliciously!

"You know, Ma'am, the police force is here to serve but we have more serious calls to answer than screaming in the bathtub at your husband. He does live at this address also, correct?"

Annie just wanted him to leave and she didn't want to be charged with anything like a "misdemeanor hysterical scream", so she apologized. But she didn't mean it. Ben actually started laughing at her after the policeman left, which was highly irritating. Anyway, the whistle warning had been instituted after that incident and worked well, as there had been no more hysterical screaming episodes.

"I thought you were working late today. Did ya'll get finished up early?"

"I'm the only one who got finished early." Annie didn't know quite where to start.

"What do you mean, Hon?"

"Oh, Ben, it's pretty bad. No, actually, it's real bad."

"Did something happen to the car?"

"Ben, for crying out loud, the car is fine. It's me. I don't know what's going to happen to me. I got escorted off the hospital parking lot by security today."

"Annie, what are you talking about? Start at the beginning." Ben sat down in the chair next to Annie's, crossed his legs, and looked at her encouragingly. So, she did what Ben said and started at the beginning – from parking in the back of the lot in the fog to walking out to the car with Max. As she told the story, it seemed to take on an even more unreal quality and she wondered if she was secretly being taped for some new reality show.

"So, I've been sitting here in this chair all day. I have no idea if I have a job or not, or even if I will have a nursing license when Nita gets through with me. The total irony of it all is that I didn't do anything wrong. Nurses make medication errors, sometimes even serious ones, and get an occurrence report. I find poor Mr. Olmos dead in the parking lot and I'm suspended."

"Annie, this is so blown out of proportion. Surely the committee who investigates it will see that and you will be back at work before you know it."

"I kept telling myself that at work today but I don't know, Ben. Remember in that movie, *Thelma and Louise*, when Thelma said, "It's like some kind of weird snowball effect."? That's how I'm starting to feel."

By the time Annie finished relating the day's events it was well past dinnertime. Ben insisted that they go out to eat and although that was the last thing she wanted to do, Annie agreed.

Mexican food definitely seemed to have some healing properties, Annie realized. Also, it was evident that her loss of appetite was short-lived. She guessed maybe she would lose her mind and her job, but not any weight after all. The chili con queso was creamy and smooth with small little bits of jalapeno, just the way she liked it. The tortillas were made there in the restaurant, and were fresh and soft. They shared an order of fajitas and a margarita. Annie rarely drank anything other than red wine because she had read the wine could possibly prevent Alzheimer's disease and she wanted to do her part to keep her mental faculties functioning at their maximum. Margaritas didn't prevent any disease but on special occasions, like getting suspended after finding a dead person in the parking lot, they did have their uses.

Ben and Annie drove home without much conversation but Annie did feel a little better. Ben was always so logical at looking at the facts and it helped to know that, logically, she should be okay pretty soon.

"Ben, I am so tired. I think I'll take a hot shower and go to bed."

"That's probably a good idea, Hon. You wait and see, you'll feel better in the morning. I know, why don't you go shopping and get a new dress?"

Ben always suggested that when he didn't know what else to say. For Ben, it was a treat to get new clothes. He simply went to the nearest store that sold men's clothes, picked out some shirts in the colors he liked, and walked up to the cashier, pulling out his credit card in one easy movement. It was a totally painless, non-stressful experience. But, as Annie had tried to explain to Ben before, shopping was not that way for her. Because of growing up where money was tight, she felt intense guilt if she bought some article of clothing that wasn't on sale. Not only did it have to be on sale, it also had to be the very best bargain in the city. Reaching this outcome was a major project, involving an intense search. Finding a dress that was the right style, color, and price often involving several days of looking and evaluating. When she did finally find " the dress", she would have to go to other stores to see if she could find the same dress cheaper. Ben just could not understand at all her mental anguish related to shopping. Annie knew that he meant well but she definitely was not going shopping tomorrow.

"Ben, I am just not up to shopping. Maybe I will drive down to the beach."

"That's a great idea, Hon. Don't worry about supper tomorrow, we'll just have eggs or grilled cheese. I'll cook."

Those were the only two foods he could manage in the kitchen, thus the menu offer was limited. Annie accepted gratefully and gave his face a gentle pat, feeling the sticky little whiskers from a day-long growth.

Before Annie could make it to the shower, the phone rang. She saw it was Christine on caller ID and hesitantly picked up the receiver.

Christine began the conversation almost before Annie could say, "Hello."

"I'm not supposed to call you. Nobody is. That's a direct order from management." Tones of intrigue filtered through the phone and Annie wondered once again about the possibility of a reality show in progress.

"Well, why are you calling then?" Annie was running on empty in the compassion department about now for anybody from the hospital, even Chris.

"Because I wanted to make sure you are okay."

"Sure, I'm fine. I just found a dead person in the parking lot who happened to be Mr. Olmos, which I couldn't tell at the time. I am suspended. Nita hates me with a vengeance and seems determined to destroy me. I may loose my job and my license. But, other than that, everything seems to be going pretty good. How about you?"

"Look, I just wanted to say I'm really sorry about what is happening to you. They had an emergency staff meeting and practically threatened anybody to not contact you while you are on suspension."

"Chris, it's okay. Thanks for calling. I'm sorry. I'm just kind of crazy right now. It was sweet of you to call and I won't tell anybody. Maybe this will get straightened out in the next three days and I'll be back."

Silence. Not a good sign.

"Chris, I have the water running for a shower. I better go. Thanks for thinking of me."

"Annie, I'm sorry . . . I want to tell you something. I think you are a good nurse."

For most people, to describe someone as a good nurse was not an expression of lavish praise, but those words coming from Chris had tremendous value. For her, that was the ultimate compliment and Annie realized that.

"Why Christine, thank you. That means a lot."

Christine had said more than she meant to and never one to dwell on feelings, said a quick goodbye. It was just as well because Annie felt as though she might start crying, one of her little habits which Christine hated.

■ ■ ■

The next day shone bright with a hot Texas sun and Annie packed some cans of Diet Coke, a PBJ sandwich, a folding chair, a murder mystery paperback, and headed down the freeway towards Galveston. She drove without the radio for a while and the silence gave her mind a pleasant empty space.

She found an empty spot of beach and pulled in. It would be packed on the weekend, but it was pretty quiet on this weekday. She slathered on plenty of sunscreen, hoping it would dry before the sand had a chance to mix with it and give her that unique sticky, prickly feeling she always remembered as a child coming to Galveston. The smooth sand felt like a cushioned rug as she walked down to the beach with her chair and mini-cooler. Packing so lightly, her little corner of the world was set up in a couple of minutes. Sitting and contemplating the water's motion, she felt that surely God had made the ocean for the purpose of calming us down when things are falling apart. The waves were steady and soothing, their rhythm echoed by the gull's whining cries overhead. Annie felt small compared to the giant ocean and her problem seemed to grow smaller, too. She remembered her Dad telling her that many things we get upset and worry about we will look back on and laugh at ten years later. While she couldn't picture ever laughing at the mess she was in now, she did see it wouldn't always be this painful. A verse from the Bible that said, "the truth shall make you free" came unbidden to her mind. That gave her courage because in all of this she had been honest and true.

The heat of the sun made the coldness of the Coke going down her throat feel absolutely wonderful after sitting for an hour or so. Walking along the beach with sand squishing between her toes, Annie found a perfect moon shell which she felt was a sign. Moon shells that didn't have little dings on the edges were extremely rare, so stumbling on a perfect one seemed quite an accomplishment.

Echoes in her mind of driving warnings from Ben ("You don't want to get caught in the late afternoon traffic, the car may overheat") told her it was time to leave. There was nothing like turning the AC on high after being in the summer sun for a couple of hours. It was almost as good as the first drink of ice-cold Diet Coke on the beach. The radio played *Hey Jude* and Annie turned the volume up and sang along with John, Paul, Ringo, and George.

Pulling into the driveway, she felt pretty good, considering. It was nice to know supper, simple though it would be, was all taken care of – courtesy of sweet Ben.

Things went pretty well till bedtime. Annie went into the bathroom right before bed, to set out her makeup on the counter for her morning routine. Mascara, eye shadow, Beauty Plus base #2 Ivory, and Barely Mocha lipstick; she had just finished, when she stopped, hand midair. What am I doing? I'm not going in tomorrow…and then a soft silent flow of tears came.

The interruption to Annie's quiet grieving was the ring of the house phone. Ben only answered his cell phone and had assigned himself off of phone duty one random day a good while ago, without any explanation or discussion. When she had pointed out the unfairness of his decision, he simply looked at her like she was speaking Martian and said, " let the answering machine get it." So she knew if she didn't hurry, she would be giving it over to the machine. It seemed so rude, like slamming the door in someone's face, maybe a friend who was nice enough to call, and Annie didn't want to turn any friend away, especially now. Catching the handset on the third ring, she looking quickly at Caller ID and, not recognizing the number, decided to chance it. But the only response to her hello was silence. After waiting a moment, she gently replaced the handset, puzzling just a bit. Was that a little mewing she had heard in the background?

6

MEMORANDUM

STATUS: PRIORITY
SUBJECT: CUSTOMER SERVICE REMINDER
TO: DAY SURGERY STAFF
FROM: NURSING MANAGEMENT
ALL NURSING STAFF ARE REQUIRED TO ATTEND
CUSTOMER SERVICE INSERVICE REVIEW. JANET WILL
SCHEDULE MEETING TIMES.
P.S. LET'S ALL REMEMBER OUR TEAM BUDDY
ATTITUDES WHEN INTERACTING WITH ANCILLARY
DEPTS. THERE HAVE BEEN SEVERAL COMPLAINTS
FROM THE LABORATORY RECENTLY.

Christine never had realized how much she depended on Annie. Without Annie here the past two days, it seemed like there was always somebody getting irritated. For instance, this afternoon she had called the lab because needed results were not back yet. The surgeon was due to arrive in an hour and she could foresee getting blamed – again.

"Where are the chemistry results on the patient Kloss? I need them now. They were done yesterday morning; they should have been back by yesterday afternoon," Christine sent a barrage of questions to the lab technician, when one question would have been enough.

"Hey, I just got here. The other lab tech is in the ER drawing stat labs, hold your horses."

Holding her horses was something Christine wasn't very good at doing.

"Listen here, the surgery is supposed to start in one hour, and if you don't find those results and fax them over – and I mean now – when the doctor comes I'll just tell him to call you, okay?"

Christine could hear the rapid shuffling of papers over the phone. "I don't see... Who drew the blood? It might have been clotted and had to be discarded."

Sensing the beginnings the game of accusation, Christine instinctively went to level one blame-avoidance mode. "Day Surgery should have been notified immediately if there was a problem with the blood. We all know how to draw blood over here, why are you saying it's our fault? It's your job to get us the results back before surgery, you know."

By this time the lab technician was done with Christine.

"Sam will be back from the ER in a few minutes. He'll call you. He's in charge." And with that, the phone clicked dead.

Christine slammed down the receiver. "What a waste of time, and that guy was so rude on top of not getting me the results." She spoke out loud to no one in particular.

Lee, Annie's replacement, walked up to the desk. "Who are you mad at now, Christine?"

"Oh, just the lab won't do its job, and they're blaming us, as usual," Christine felt her jaw tighten and she wondered if another headache was not coming on. She had sure been having more of them lately, especially in the last two days.

Lee seemed uninterested in Christine's assessment of the problems. She walked off without response towards the waiting room.

Within minutes, she returned bringing a patient back. As his wheelchair squeaked past, she heard him ask, " Where's Annie? She's always my nurse when I come in."

It was Mr. Allen, the grouchy old man who was on dialysis. He had returned to have a toe amputated on his remaining good leg. Christine glanced up, and saw he looked about the same as she remembered him. Disheveled and still unwashed, she guessed from the aroma she detected when he went by.

Christine couldn't believe what she heard Lee telling him. "Oh, Annie's in trouble. She's on suspension."

"What the hell are you talking about, girl? That is one of the best nurses I know," Mr. Allen slapped his hand down on the armrest of his wheel chair, and for just a minute Christine thought he had slapped Lee. When she turned around, she realized that the sound had been harmless. But she couldn't believe Lee had told a patient that kind of information. That was totally inappropriate and had to be addressed. Christine stood up and walked straight into the room.

"Lee, come to the desk, now." Christine turned and left.

"What's the problem?" Lee seemed genuinely surprised.

"The problem is you. What do you think you are doing, telling a patient about Annie?"

Lee shrugged her shoulders. "It's the truth. Why shouldn't I tell him? That's what happens when you break the rules. I'm sorry, but that's just life."

Christine doubted very much that Lee was sorry. She seemed to take pleasure in pointing out what she considered to be Annie's blame. "Well, you shouldn't tell patients things like that, that's all."

"Who put you in charge of telling me what to say?" Lee's voice was raised and she turned away quickly, marching back into the patient's room.

Why is everybody being so rude to me? All I am doing is my job. But at some level, Christine knew that if Annie had been here, she would have smoothed things over and gotten the lab results without threats. She would have made one of her funny little jokes to the lab tech and Lee wouldn't be storming off mad right now. The sound of voices raised in anger interrupted Christine's thoughts. It was Mr. Allen yelling at Lee.

"I'm telling you this one more time, and that's it. I am not taking my pants off. It's too hard to get out of this wheelchair and my foot hurts too much. Damn it – do it like Annie does it!"

Lee wasn't about to be coerced into changing her procedure to fit Annie's routine which, coincidentally, was against policy. "Absolutely no way, Mr. Allen, you have to be in a hospital gown to go to surgery. I don't know what you mean about 'Annie's way', but you are going to have to get out of those clothes now, that's all there is to it."

Mr. Allen had been a patient too many times to be intimidated by a nurse.

"Well, you just write on your little chart, "the patient refused" because I'm damn sure refusing, you got it?"

Much to her surprise, Christine found herself getting up and walking calmly into the fray. "Lee, it's okay. I'll sign off Mr. Allen's chart." *Annie, this one's for you.*

Lee looked up, in surprise. "This patient is refusing to . . ."

"Yes, I know. I could hear the conversation from the desk. I'll take over with Mr. Allen." Christine knew that when Mr. Allen got to the operating room area and still had his pants on she would probably get reported and blamed for not following policy, but it just didn't seem that important right now.

Lee shook her head and exited the room. Though unintended, the consequences of her actions had gotten her out of a messy situation.

Mr. Allen wasn't quite sure what Christine's plans were and began cursing to get his dominance established. A string of expletives directed to the room in general, filled the air with bits of obscenities that floated around like dust specks in the light. When he stopped to take a breath, Christine was able to speak.

"It's okay, Mr. Allen. I'll help you just change out of your shirt and we'll put the hospital gown on. Then when you get to the operating room they can change your pants when they put you on the stretcher. Is that the way Annie did it?"

"Damn right, it is. She must have told you how to take care of me, huh?"

"Yes, Mr. Allen, as a matter of fact, she did."

■ ■ ■

Nita shut the desk drawer with a jarring thud. There was no one else in the office to hear it. She knew she should go home. She was too tired to do any more on the budget project Mr. Evans had assigned her. It was just so hard to leave something unfinished.

As she got up and turned off the lights, she shivered. Why was the hospital always so cold at night? Every thermostat control in the place was encased in a plastic lock box, making any adjustments impossible. The only person with the power to change the temperature was the all-powerful maintenance man who held the key. "Why does the maintenance man have the key and I can't have one?" Nita had voiced the question once at a management meeting. The question was brushed off with a laugh. Of course, the other nursing supervisors just paged maintenance when they wanted the temperature changed. But Nita had noticed that often Maintenance didn't answer her pages – especially Max, since the incident with that nurse in Day Surgery. No matter, Nita was prepared for any temperature change. A sweater was always folded up in the bottom drawer of her desk, as well as an umbrella just waiting for the first raindrop. Not one had fallen for several weeks now. The cracks in the lawn's surface at the edge of the sidewalk were evidence of that. But the unexpected was something Nita was always waiting for, like a cat at a mouse hole.

As she walked down the hallway past the other darkened administration offices, Nita relished the feeling of martyrdom (I'm the only truly dedicated person in this place) for a few moments. It would be nice to have a Security escort to her car in the dark parking lot, but Max was probably off somewhere having one more in a long series of coffee breaks. Plus, he wouldn't answer her page anyway. Never mind him, she could manage getting to her car alone. She was used to doing things alone. Nita had attended self-defense classes. She knew to walk briskly, look assertive, and have car keys in hand, ready to gouge the unsuspecting attacker's eyes or private parts. Still, after making it safely to the car it was a relief to actually push the locks down, closing the door with a loud thud.

"Look out for this one," the radio shouted out as she turned the engine on, causing her to gasp a sharp intake of air. The announcer was warning of a fast-moving line of thunderstorms, causing Nita to let out a little "damn" as she realized she hadn't taken the umbrella out of the drawer. But as the announcer continued, she heard the storms were approaching San Antonio, not Houston.

Entering her apartment, she glanced at the clock to see it was almost midnight. It had been a long day and she would return to the hospital promptly at 8:00 AM in the morning. The soft "mew-mew" of Amanda greeted her as the little yellow cat hurried to welcome her home. Nita reached down, scooped her up and they nuzzled each other in affection. As the cat purred, Nita made little humming sounds back, a human version of her cat's greeting. Amanda followed Nita silently as she performed her ritual search, under the bed and in each closet, to rule out any possibility of an intruder in waiting. To Amanda, this funny little game her owner played each time she came home was part of playtime. She would run under the bed when Nita stooped down to search and then run to the closet to jump in when the door was opened for inspection. It was only after her search was completed that Nita relaxed her tight grip on the keys and put them up on the little hook right by the front door. The apartment was clean and shiny, as anyone who knew Nita would have expected. The one unusual thing a casual observer might notice is that the walls were completely bare of any personal effects – no family portraits, not even any snapshots sitting on the small tables on either side of the couch. The only identifying evidence of Nita's tenancy was her nursing diploma, matted perfectly and hanging over the small kitchen table. If the diploma and Amanda were removed, no one would know Nita lived here. Only the apartment maintenance man had ever seen either of those things. Oh, yes, and the cable man. Cable was one luxury in Nita's life. The weather channel was wonderful.

Quickly into her gown, she lay back on the pillow, her eyes becoming heavy almost immediately. Amanda curled up on the pillow beside her and purred loudly. Nita gently scratched her behind her soft ears. They were both dozing off together when suddenly Anna Brown's face ran across her last bit of consciousness. She was jarred to awareness, as if Anna had come into the room and thrown cold water on her.

Nita sat up in bed and turned on the lamp beside her. She reached in the drawer and pulled out a pack of cigarettes. She lit up and inhaled with the practiced ease of years of experience. The only place she ever smoked was in bed, breaking the cardinal rule, but she was focused on the other rules, the hospital rules that Anna Brown had broken, and broken in a big way.

"Why, Amanda, why does that nurse keep breaking the rules? And she never seems to get punished, just says 'sorry' and goes merrily on her way." Mashing the cigarette to a crushed wad and twisting it over and over, Annie would not have liked the look that was in Nita's eyes now. But the little yellow cat was oblivious and responded by relocating to Nita's lap and gently rubbing her cold nose against Nita's neck. She was used to these late-night questions from her owner – just part of another game.

7

MEMORANDUM

STATUS: PRIORITY
SUBJECT: POLICY AND PROCEDURE BOOK
TO: ALL NURSING STAFF
FROM: NURSING MANAGEMENT
PLEASE REMEMBER THE POLICY AND PROCEDURE BOOK IS YOUR GUIDE FOR ACCURACY IN YOUR JOB. REFER TO IT AND IT ONLY, WHEN YOU NEED TO KNOW THE PROPER GUIDELINES FOR A PROCEDURE. NOTE: THE P&P IS CURRENTLY BEING REVISED AND REVIEWED FOR ENTRY ON-LINE, SO ALL PROCEDURES MAY NOT BE COMPLETELY ACCURATE OR CURRENT. PLEASE BEAR WITH US DURING THIS TIME OF TRANSITION.

ate in the afternoon of the third day of suspension, Janet made the call Annie had been waiting for.

"Annie, I just got off the phone with the investigative committee. You are coming back to Day Surgery – tomorrow. "

"Wow, Janet, that's great. Thanks so much for calling me as soon as you found out. This waiting and not knowing that everything is okay has been tough, but Ben kept telling me that after they heard all the facts . . ."

Janet interrupted, "Annie, everything is not all okay yet. I'm sorry. You can't have any contact with patients until a final decision has been reached. I wish things were different, but don't worry, I'll keep you busy."

"What do you mean, Janet? Taking care of patients is what I do. What else am I supposed to do?"

"Well, I am making space for you in my office. The hospital policy and procedure book has to be reviewed and proof-read before it is put on line. You will be working on that in the morning. Then at 2:00 pm you will meet with the peer review committee. They want to interview you, which shouldn't take too long. We will wait on their decision to see if you can go back to patient care. Try not to worry, and let's just do what they say and hopefully everything will be back to normal before you know it."

"I'm forgetting what normal is. Oh well, what are my hours tomorrow?"

"Well, it doesn't matter too much, since you are not doing patient . . ." Janet stopped herself mid-sentence. "Why don't you come in at 8:00? I'll meet you in my office then and show you where I filed the policy book."

"Okay, I'll see you then."

"Annie, I'm glad you'll be back with us. I've missed you. Your co-workers have, too."

As she clicked the phone off, Annie sighed. "Gee, just what I've always wanted – to proofread the policy and procedure book. Maybe I'll get to work on the computer some, too. Maybe Nita will drop by for coffee to make my day complete."

■ ■ ■

Ben came in whistling *Blue Skies Smiling at Me*, which let Annie know he was in what Annie called his "psychotic-optimistic" mode. When he was in this mode, there was no such thing as bad news. If Annie had told him her right leg fell off, he would say, "Isn't it great you have a left leg to fall back on". Sure enough, when she told him of Janet's phone call he responded with, "See, I told you you'd be going back to work. Don't worry. I bet after this peer committee meets, it's all going to be over."

"It's not like I haven't had a reason to feel a tad negative, Ben. You would be a basket case if this happened to you, so back off a little and stop whistling."

Ben realized he'd carried his optimism a little too far, too fast. "Annie, I'm sorry, it's just that I'm not used to you being so down and I want everything to be okay. Forgive me?"

"I guess so, Ben. I can't really afford to stay mad at you. You are one of the few in my not-very-crowded corner right now. I'm not even sure if Janet is on my side."

"She is, Annie. Just remember she's still in management. But you've always said how kind and fair she is."

"You're right, as usual. This whole thing has made me kind of paranoid. But remember, Ben, just because you're paranoid doesn't mean people aren't out to get you."

Ben reached over and tousled her hair, trying to be affectionate. Annie grimaced inwardly because she had just finished washing and blow-drying it and her hair only had a short life-span for looking good. Then it deteriorated to a certain unique flimsiness, curling up at odd places and lying totally flat in others. Ben had just helped that process along but of course he was completely unaware, being a man who only had to comb his hair once in the morning. Another of life's little inequities – men's hair versus women's hair.

In spite of waiting an eternal three days in suspension-land, somehow the next morning seemed to arrive too quickly. When Annie pulled into the parking lot, she carefully parked in the front row. She looked neither to the right or left as she got out of the car. Head held high and looking through the sunlight at the professional building, she was so intent on not looking down and discovering so much as a dead fly, she tripped on an old soft drink can and had to catch herself to keep from falling. She had missed her co-workers and her job a lot and yet, at the same time, was dreading that first contact. It reminded her of how she felt on a hot summer day, right before she submerged her body in the swimming pool. The coldness of the water was painful, though relief from the heat made it worth the pain.

When she reached the time clock, no one else was there. Most had already clocked in and were taking care of patients. But of course, she wasn't able to do that anymore. Feeling like a leper, she walked down the back hall to Janet's office. Janet was already sitting at her desk and turned with a big smile.

"Welcome back, Annie! You look good. I brought some doughnuts fresh from Shipley's to share with you. See, I have a chair and a spot just for you."

As Janet gave the chair seat a little welcoming touch, Annie felt like a kid on her first day to school and was half expecting Janet to set out some crayons and a coloring book.

The doughnuts really were fresh, though; soft and squishy with the sugar glaze drippy and sweet – all the attributes of a true comfort food. Soon she was set up with the giant hospital policy and procedure book in front of her. This book had a listing of instructions for every imaginable procedure that could be performed on a patient. Beginning with "Taking an Oral Temperature", it was basic to the point of insulting one's intelligence. The first instruction on the temperature procedure was: "remove thermometer from holder." Gee, couldn't you just insert the thermometer AND holder into the patient's mouth? It was going to be a long day.

After a couple of hours, Annie's eyes were starting to get heavy. She wasn't used to sitting motionless for extended periods.

"Janet, I'm going to run to the lounge and get a cup of coffee. I'll be right back."

"The lounge is fine, Annie. Just be sure you don't go through any patient areas. They were very specific in their instructions about no patient contact."

Yes, you never know, I might accidentally touch a patient, and who knows what could happen.

As she pushed open the lounge door, animated conversations suddenly hushed. She tried to think of something funny to announce her entrance. Brain activity low, as had been the case a lot lately, no humorous words formed, so she resorted to the always available banal, " Hi everyone, good to see you,"(as if she had just returned from a fun-filled vacation.)

People starting chiming in together, welcoming her back, saying she was missed, but carefully avoiding any meaningful conversation (instructions from management, no doubt). Annie had planned on sitting down in the lounge for her coffee, but instead poured it quickly and offered her apologies for not staying. "I'm working in Janet's office today, so I better get back. See y'all later."

As she walked back towards the office, she almost bumped into Dr. March.

"Annie, hello, it's so good to see you back. Is everything all resolved?"

Annie hesitated a moment, unsure of how much Dr. March knew of the situation. Sensing her reluctance, Dr. March added, "It's okay. Christine told me what happened to you. I haven't said anything to anyone else. I was hoping it would all be resolved after the investigative committee met. Did that not happen?"

"I am allowed back to work, but I can't have any patient contact. I am working in Janet's office on paper work. I meet with the peer review committee at 2:00 pm today, so maybe something will be finalized then. Thanks for asking. I am not supposed to talk about it to anybody, that's all."

"Annie, do you have a lawyer?" Dr. March looked way too serious.

"No, I hadn't even thought about it. Why?"

"Annie, you need to have one – to protect your interests. The hospital is not interested in your protection; it is interested in protecting itself from a megabucks lawsuit. If the ship is going down, they will throw you under the bus."

Annie smiled at Dr. March's mixed metaphor.

Misinterpreting the smile, Dr. March continued, "Annie, I'm serious here. I know an attorney who has handled a case for a fellow physician. I will be more than happy to contact him for you."

"Well, I don't know, do you think that's necessary? It sounds so extreme to me. I didn't do anything wrong."

"No, I'm sure you didn't, but sometimes not doing anything wrong is not enough to keep from getting sued. I don't want to scare you, but I really think you need to talk to him."

Annie stood, wondering how much attorney fees would be and where the money would come from. Although she and Ben were not poor, they had just had a major house repair due to termites and that had left them temporarily strapped.

As if she were psychic, Dr. March said, "Annie, I am going to pay the first thousand dollars of the fee. It is not a loan; it is helping a friend out. This is not open for discussion. I am going to call him when I get through with cases today, and I'll get back to you, okay?"

Tears started coming and Annie couldn't even speak. Dr. March hugged her. Just as she did, her beeper went off simultaneously. It was a stat page, and she turned to jog towards the source of the emergency. Annie's brain finally functioned enough to call out, "Thank you . . . so much . . . not just the money" as Dr. March disappeared around the corner.

The thought of seeing an attorney was almost as scary as the peer review committee meeting coming up in a few hours. But Dr. March's concern and care had touched Annie deeply. She had been the first one not afraid to talk honestly to Annie since this mess all happened.

Settling in for some more fascinating reading through the hospital policy and procedure book, it was only a few minutes before the door to

Janet's office opened. In came Christine and Teresa, almost rushing towards Annie.

" Why, darlin', welcome back, I missed you so much," Teresa's warm words were quickly accompanied by an all-engulfing hug that made Annie's chair tilt backwards.

As Teresa continued to tell Annie how much she missed her, Christine simply walked over and stood beside her. She extended her hand and patted Annie's shoulder over and over again. The touch was so light it was almost undetectable, yet Annie felt those soft pats intensely, and she couldn't keep back some tears.

"Thanks, ya'll, it feels so good to know you are on my side. I get to feeling so alone, sometimes . . ." Annie had to leave the sentence dangling while she tried to get control of herself. She didn't want to upset Christine by dissolving into weeping, which could happen pretty easily, about now.

Janet, trying to lighten the atmosphere, said suddenly, "okay, every-body, group hug."

Annie had to inwardly chuckle at that. Group hugs were definitely one of Christine's least favorite activities. But she staunchly gathered into their small circle and stiffly tightened her arms in her best imitation of a hug. Though it was kind of corny, it was sweet. It did help everyone to get on the other side of the emotional heaviness that had infused the room like a big spray of room freshener.

"Time for me to play boss, everybody back to work," Janet interjected. "Hopefully, Annie will be back where she belongs before you know it." Janet was ending the spontaneous support session with a dose of reality. The unit was busy today, and Teresa and Christine were being missed.

"Maybe we can all have lunch together, Annie. Call when you can take your break and we'll try to take ours, too," Teresa called over her shoulder as she and Christine left the office.

That sounded wonderful to Annie. She was feeling much stronger just having some friends wanting to be with her. But when she called about a lunch break, things were hectic in pre-op and neither Teresa nor Christine could get away. Annie, in an unusual burst of organization, had actually packed a lunch. She was glad because she really didn't want to go the lounge. People in general, seemed to feel uncomfortable around her and that discomfort was highly contagious. As she cleared a little space at the desk, shoving aside the huge black vinyl policy and procedure book, the aloneness felt like a pleasant companion. *Hello darkness, my old friend.*

But soon her mind started drifting forward to the upcoming peer review committee meeting. It lay ahead of her like a dreaded dental appointment. Annie had never been to a peer review committee meeting, although she knew one or two nurses who had. In their cases, each had made a serious medication error. The committee was composed of several staff nurses and one nursing supervisor. One would think that other nurses would be somewhat understanding when a fellow nurse had made a mistake. But the two nurses who had been through the process had both told Annie pretty much the same story. The committee members seemed to enjoy judgment and punishment. Annie remembered a saying that she had heard before, "Nurses eat their own", and guessed there was some truth to that. Very unlike physicians who were loathe to criticize or report another physician. Why the difference was a mystery, probably something to do with power, money, or the male-female factor, she decided. Almost all the weird, unfair things in nursing came down to one of these three factors. Somebody should do a study on that for their master's thesis. Nobody ever will, though; it's just one of those things about nursing one has to put up with. The Snickers bar, her dessert, didn't taste as comforting as chocolate should. When she realized this, she felt even more anxious. Chocolate was one of Annie's major anti-anxiety medications. Like aspirin, it's properties were not fully understood; but like aspirin, it almost always helped.

The phone rang. Janet was at another of the endless meetings she had to attend. Annie answered the phone using the hospital approved greeting. But here in the quiet, unhurried office, she spoke at a comprehensible rate instead of running all the words into one giant word, like she usually did.

"Good afternoon, Trenton James General Hospital, this is Day Surgery, Janet Simmon's office. Annie Brown, RN speaking. How may I help you?"

"Hey Annie, this is Teresa. There is a friend of yours in the Emergency Room. The ER nurse called here to let you know."

"My goodness, who is it?"

"A Mrs. Lindsey, she said."

"That's my next-door neighbor. Is she okay?"

"I think she's having some shortness of breath."

"Thanks for telling me, Teresa. I'll go check on her."

Annie felt sure it would be within the rules to visit a friend in the hospital, since she wasn't going as a nurse. Also, conveniently, there was no one around for her to ask permission to go.

As she walked to the ER, she realized she hadn't seen Mrs. Lindsey in several weeks. She hoped it was nothing serious. Mrs. Lindsey was such a sweet little lady. She was a widow from England and one of her loves was her garden. She had a beautiful British accent and grew beautiful roses, and every so often there would be a small tap at Annie's front door. Mrs. Lindsey would be there offering a bouquet of her roses, "to such a dear lady as you, Annie." Annie admired the roses so much. Mrs. Lindsey had given her cuttings more than once and Annie had promptly killed each one with too much or too little water. After several tries, Mrs. Lindsey and Annie decided it was better for Mrs. Lindsey to grow the roses and Annie to get to enjoy them.

She rounded a long hallway to the ER and found a passing nurse to point her to Mrs. Lindsey's room. When she entered, she was shocked. Mrs. Lindsey was on a stretcher, sitting up with oxygen going and still struggling to breathe. Her color was ashen and she had the telltale look of fear in her eyes, which so often came with extreme shortness of breath. She looked to have lost weight, too, since Annie had seen her.

"Annie, it's you, dear," Mrs. Lindsey flashed a smile, in spite of her distress.

"Mrs. Lindsey, I just got the message that you were here and I came right over. What happened?" Annie gently grasped her friend's hand through the side rails. It was cold and damp to her touch.

"I'm not really sure. I've just been so tired lately and then it seemed like it was harder and harder to catch my breath and . . ." Mrs. Lindsey had to stop and rest before she could go on.

" Don't try to talk too much. Do you need me to do anything for you?"

"Yes, dear if you could. When you get home, could you check on Miss Prissy? You remember where the key is, under the rock in the big blue flower pot. I left her plenty of food and water, but she will be worrying about me. Just tell her that I'm going to be fine and I will be home soon. And if you could check my mail, that would be great, dear." Mrs. Lindsey may have had some more things to say, but she didn't have any more oxygen to say them with.

"No problem. I'll take care of Miss Prissy 'till you get home and the mail too. I can water the flowers if you want."

It was a sign of true trust for Mrs. Lindsey to turn the care of her flowers over to the flower-killer, Annie Brown. But she nodded willingly.

Annie stood there with tears in her eyes. She was worried about her little neighbor going downhill so fast.

"Is there anybody you want me to call for you to let them know you're sick?"

Mrs. Lindsey said softly, "there's no one, dear."

Just then the door opened and a nurse came in with a clipboard.

"Honey, I need you to sign some papers. It's a consent for the specialist to do that test on your lungs, remember?"

"Mrs. Lindsey nodded and tried to scoot to a full upright position, but didn't have the strength.

"Here, I'll help." Annie volunteered to the nurse. With a nurse on either side, on the count of three they both lifted and Mrs. Lindsey was almost propelled out of the bed.

"Whoops, I guess we didn't realize our own strength," Annie smiled to the ER nurse.

"Mrs. Lindsey, do you remember the doctor explained the test to look into your lungs to see what the matter is?"

"Yes, my dear, where do I sign?" Mrs. Lindsey graciously took the pen and smiled to Annie.

"This nice doctor I talked to is a lung specialist, so I think that will be alright, don't you?" She looked to Annie for approval.

"Well, yes, I guess so Mrs. Lindsey. There sure is some reason you are having so much trouble breathing, so it's probably a good idea to see what's going on." To the ER nurse, she asked, "Is she having a bronchoscopy?"

"Umhum. Sign here please. We've got to get you ready. They've got an open spot on the surgery schedule.

"Mrs. Lindsey, I better go. I'll check on you later. You're going to get better soon."

Annie leaned over and gave Mrs. Lindsey a quick kiss on her forehead.

As she walked out of the room, she almost collided with Dr. Nagel coming towards the room. He leaned around the doorway and called in to Mrs. Lindsey,

"Okay, ma'am, we are going to get this checked out in no time. I'll see you upstairs in the operating room."

Annie walked away with a sick feeling in her stomach. Why did it have to be him doing the bronchoscopy? She thought of Mrs. Nguyen and her complications because of his lousy technique.

And when Mrs. Lindsey asked me, I told her sure, go ahead get this done. Why didn't I think to look and see who was doing it? What can I do now? If I go back and tell her don't do it and she gets worse, it will be my fault. But if I don't do something and she gets a pneumothorax because of him, I couldn't live with myself.

She heard someone calling out for a nurse and turned around. It was Mrs. Lindsey's nurse, trying to catch up to her.

She handed Annie the necklace that Mrs. Lindsey always wore, a plain gold chain with a small gold heart.

"Could you take her jewelry for her? She asked me to give it to you to keep for her. She said for you to wear it."

"Sure, tell her I'll take good care of it." Oh, great – a reminder of how awful a friend I am. She stopped and carefully put the necklace on and closed the clasp.

What could she do? Annie knew that her options were very limited, especially with her situation right now. But at least she could page Janet and ask her. As she slowly walked down the hallway, she passed the surgery transportation staff on the way to pick up Mrs. Lindsey.

For once, why couldn't they be running late, so I could have some time to figure something out?

She went directly to the office and paged Janet. Janet called back right away and Annie explained how scared she was for her friend to be operated on by Dr. Nagel.

"Annie, I understand your concerns, but legally there is nothing you can do. Dr. Nagel is licensed to do surgery here. You can't go in and tell your friend that you don't trust him. That is not ethical conduct. There is a board he has to answer to if he has too many complications."

"Yeah, but that didn't do that Vietnamese patient, Mrs. Nguyen, any good. She got a pneumothorax and ended up in ICU, remember?"

"But not all of his patients have complications, you know. You are just focusing on the ones who do. I've got to go now. I'll be back to the office in a few minutes."

Janet was probably right. It's not like he went around killing patients, after all. She had just gotten back to the office when the door opened and Janet walked in.

"Annie, I'm sorry about your friend and Dr. Nagel. It's just that you know and I know there is nothing we can do at this point. But I think you are under stress right now and you are getting things out of proportion. She's going to be okay."

"It's just that she is such a sweet little lady. She doesn't have anybody but her cat and her roses that she brings me sometime, Janet, and she trusts me," Annie put her head down and cried.

Janet came over and gave Annie a hug.

"I know this is a rough time for you. I wish I had a better answer."

"Sometimes there just aren't any easy answers. But you are right, she will probably be fine."

"There you go. Don't you need to get over to the peer review meeting?"

Annie's eyes were nice and swollen and red. Her nose was starting to drip. This is not the way she wanted to appear before the committee.

"I don't even know what room they are meeting in, do you?"

"Yes, it would probably be good if you were there at least 15 minutes early, in case they are running ahead of schedule. They are meeting in the conference room on the third floor. If you want to leave now, that's fine. Check with me when you get back so I know what to do with you."

Feeling as if she were like a bothersome recurring rash to Janet, Annie got up slowly, closing the policy and procedure book. As she turned to leave, she had to ask one more question.

"Janet, would you let Dr. Nagel do surgery on you?"

Janet just looked at Annie sheepishly and the unspoken answer passed between them.

She found the third floor conference room with plenty of time to spare. The door was closed and there was a row of three chairs sitting along the wall beside it. One of the chairs was occupied by a nurse that Annie didn't know, but recognized as one of the nurses who worked on the surgical floor. She gave Annie a tight smile, and said, "You are supposed to knock on the door so they know you are here."

Annie complied with a brief soft knock along with the completely irrational wish that no one was home, just as she wished many years ago when she tried to sell Girl Scout cookies. Of course someone was at home. The door opened a crack and another nurse Annie didn't recognize peeked out. Only her eyes were visible, as if Annie were possibly a dangerous intruder who would break the imaginary safety chain with a single snap and burst in with a drawn gun. "Name?" she requested.

"Annie Brown. I am supposed to be here at 2:00, but I came over a little early because I thought you might need me early or something . . ." Annie realized as the words started pouring out that she was nervous and rambling.

"Yes, I know who's scheduled. Just take a seat." The door closed abruptly. *Hmm, that went well.*

Sitting down by the other "waitee", she tried to be friendly. When she got nervous she inevitably tried to be humorous, and it generally backfired on her. However that never seemed to deter her.

"What are you in for?"

"I made two medication errors in two months, I guess that is over the limit or something. I bet those nurses in there have made more that two med errors, so they shouldn't think they are better than me." She seemed angry at having been called to account.

Annie thought that two medication errors in two months was quite a lot, but decided now was not the time to give her opinion.

"What did you do?" The other nurse looked hopefully at Annie, maybe wishing that Annie had made three med errors or worse.

" Well, it's kind of complicated," Annie started out, "I was coming to work last week. Remember that really foggy morning? And I had to use my husband's car and he wanted me to park on the back row so his car wouldn't get scratched . . ."

By this time, as Annie looked over at the yet un-named nurse, she was met with an expression of wonder and Annie realized she was rambling again. At this point, she began to wish she had never initiated conversation but before she could start rambling some more, the door opened and a name was called.

"Mrs. Andrews, please." Mrs. Andrews got up. Annie gave her a quick whispered "good luck" as the nurse turned to enter the room. The door closed with a loud click, firmly closing Mrs. Andrews in with the peer review committee.

Annie longed to put her ear to the door but knew that she would be instantly discovered, the way her luck had been running. As she sat waiting, trying to calm her mind, she kept reminding herself to tell the truth and let the facts speak. That was Ben's advice to her that morning and she held onto it tightly as the minutes passed.

After a fifteen-minute wait, the door to the conference room opened. Nurse Andrews exited, looking pale and showing telltale red, swollen eyelids, which revealed her recent tears. Annie started to speak but before she could, Mrs. Andrews brushed past. Immediately the guard nurse called out, "Mrs. Brown, you are next."

She took a deep breath, entered the room, and surveyed the faces. Of the five staff nurses seated at the large table, she recognized three of them as nurses from the surgical floor where she occasionally delivered patients. That was a positive sign. Hopefully they remembered her as a good nurse who cared about her patients. Of course, all these encouraging signs were negated when she saw the identity of the nurse manager, non other than Nita. *This could be bad, this could be very bad.* Annie glanced at Nita's face, but her eyes were directed downward toward her ever-present clipboard.

"Mrs. Brown, you are here today as a result of an incident last week which is classified as a Code 13. We have read the report and have a few questions to ask," the door guard nurse was the sole speaker thus far. She was one of the nurses totally unfamiliar to Annie. Built square and strong, she had a firm jaw and bore a striking resemblance to a wrestler. Annie realized she was very nervous and tried taking slow deep breaths as she waited for questions. Her knees felt shaky and she asked if she could sit down. The guard nurse gave a nod and as Annie pulled the chair across the floor, a long high-pitched squeak was emitted, breaking the silence like a burp in church. Nita looked up at this sound and their eyes met for a blink, too brief a time for Annie to get a read on Nita.

The guard nurse spoke. "Mrs. Brown, please describe what you did when you first discovered the body."

Annie carefully cast back in her mind and related the facts as accurately as she could.

"So the reason you didn't start CPR was that you felt the body was too cool, and the person had been dead for a while? Is that correct?"

"Yes, I felt it would have been not only futile, but wrong."

Nita spoke up, "What about your statement to me that you thought he may have been murdered and that this was a crime scene and you didn't want to move anything?"

Annie realized she had forgotten that part of her thought processes. Now, here in the committee room, it really did sound melodramatic and unbelievable. "Well yes, that thought did cross my mind. It was so dark and hard to see because of the fog, it was just hard to assess the situation, I guess."

"But you didn't see any blood, or a gun or knife, or anything to indicate that this was a crime scene, did you?"

"No, no, nothing like that, it's just that I was trying to quickly run through all the possibilities and that crossed my mind, but it wouldn't have changed my decision or my actions. No matter what the cause, he had been dead for some time." Annie wasn't sure, but she thought she saw one or two of the heads nod slightly, as if in agreement.

The guard nurse wrote a little note and passed it up to Nita who quickly scanned it and said, "Okay."

The guard nurse then spoke in a rather kindly tone, "We are sure it was a very difficult experience for you, Mrs. Brown. Thank you for answering our questions openly. You may return to your unit. We will contact your manager within the hour with our recommendation."

Annie scooted the chair back out to get up. Again, heavy squeaks cut the silence. One of the nurses stifled a small chuckle.

Annie didn't know whether one should say thank you or not in a situation like this (does the accused thank her accusers?), but she mumbled a soft thanks as she left just to be on the safe side of etiquette.

All in all, that went rather well. Annie made her way back to Janet's office. *I think most of those nurses understood what I was facing and saw how hard it was to figure out what to do. Plus, I still wouldn't do anything differently if I had it to do all over again. Well, I wouldn't tell Nita that stuff about it maybe being a murder and crime scene, that's all.*

Janet looked up expectantly as Annie entered the office. "How did everything go?" Annie related the gist of things to Janet and told her to expect a call today from the committee.

"Well, that's great Annie. Are you feeling better about things?"

"Maybe I shouldn't but yes, I do. I felt that most of the other nurses in there understood how I made my decision."

"I guess for now, just keep plugging away on the policy and procedure book until we hear something."

"Right. I can hang on a page or two longer, I guess," Annie pulled the massive book open again. "Oh, yes, I promised Ben I would call him as soon as I was out of the meeting. I'll make it quick."

"Sure, go ahead. I am waiting for a call or I would step out . . ."

"No, that's fine, Janet. You already know what I'm going to tell him."

"Honey, that sounds great." Annie could already imagine a whistling tune coming on from Ben – it was in his voice. I'm sure you are going to be cleared within the hour. Let's go out to eat tonight to celebrate," Ben was always looking for an excuse for a margarita.

"Well, nothing is final yet but I should know within the hour. Yes, that sounds good. Gotta go, the policy and procedure book calls, love you."

"I love you more, Annie. See you around 5:30."

Ben was so good. Annie made a mental note to tell him so when she saw him.

The phone rang with a jarring tone a few minutes later. Janet answered with the required greeting, "Trenton James General Hospital, Day Surgery, Janet, how may I help you?"

Annie gave up all pretense of being polite and stared at Janet's facial expression, looking for clues. But Janet said nothing in response except "Alright, I will comply and let Annie know the findings. Bye."

"Well, can I close up the policy and procedure book and get back to work?"

"I'm afraid I have some bad news. The peer review committee has recommended that your case go to the state board for review. You are still not allowed to have contact with patients until that happens. They are faxing the report to the state board of nursing today and will let us know when the hearing will take place." Janet was talking in a monotone, as if she were dictating a report, and avoiding all eye contact.

Annie sat unmoving, unable to actually understand all that Janet was saying. She could see her mouth moving but the words were all jumbled together, the static in her brain drowning them out. "Are you saying it's not all over? I don't understand what you mean. What does the state board have to do with this?"

"Annie, I really don't understand why they are doing this, maybe to avoid a lawsuit or something, but I will go with you, you won't be alone." Janet meant well but Annie knew that even if fifty people went with her, she was alone.

"I need to take a walk or something to absorb this. I can't focus on the policy and procedure book anymore right now."

"Annie, if you need to take the rest of the day off, that's fine with me. I know this is a big shock to you and frankly, to me, too."

There was nothing Annie would have liked more than to LEAVE THIS PLACE, but she thought she might need to save her vacation hours. No telling how short her paycheck might get through all this mess. "Thanks a lot, Janet, but I think I'll be okay after a walk. This is my reality now and I have to learn to live with it until it is all finally settled. I shouldn't have been so optimistic with Nita on the committee. I know, I just know that some of those nurses were on my side. Anyway, I guess there is no way to appeal the peer committee findings, is there?"

"Not that I know of, but I will check on that while you are taking your walk."

Annie got up slowly. The strength seemed totally drained out of her. It was as if a huge wave had hit her unaware, pulling her under, surrounding her so completely that her feet dangled loosely unable to touch the bottom. Instinctively, she took a deep breath. Janet got up and came over to her, giving her shoulders a squeeze.

"Try not to worry, Annie. You'll get through this, I know you will."

"Janet, I keep trying not to worry. I tell myself that I didn't do anything wrong, so I have nothing to fear, but it just doesn't seem to help."

"I know you have had a string of negative things lately, but it's got to get better."

Annie wasn't in the mood to get cheered up right now. "I'll be back in a few minutes."

The hospital was no place for a private time anywhere, but Annie was determined. She headed out the doors of the professional building towards the far edge of the parking lot. There was a tree on one of the corners. Of course, it wasn't a very big tree. The spot of shade it provided was just about big enough for her dog, Bear. Annie scrunched in the tiny shade and sat down, hoping no fire ants were in the vicinity. She looked up through the leaves and asked God what she had done wrong. He didn't say anything, but after a few minutes she remembered that doing the right thing had meant that Jesus wound up hanging on a cross. Realizing that doing the right thing didn't always protect you from bad things happening and seeing this come into perspective more clearly lifted her spirits, even if only a little. Suddenly she felt a sharp stinging on her ankle. Sure enough, it was one of those dratted fire ants. "Thanks for letting me know my break is over." After her gracious thanks to the ant, she pinched him to death and got up before any of his relatives showed up on the scene to avenge his merciless killing.

Walking back into Janet's office, Annie felt she could face the policy and procedure book again and get through the day. "I'm better now, Janet. I will be okay."

"That's my Annie," Janet responded a little too cheerfully, in Annie's opinion. "I have to leave for a meeting across town, so you'll have the office to yourself for the rest of the day. I'll see you in the morning, then," she said as she gathered her belongings into the ubiquitous canvas bag all nurses seemed to possess. The door shut with a quiet click and Annie returned to the giant black vinyl book. "Drawing a blood sample – 1. Wash hands, using antibacterial soap." What a novel idea, to wash your hands in antibacterial soap! What would they think of next? Annie proceeded on to another fun-filled afternoon with the insanity of the policy and procedure book.

She had decided not to call Ben back. She would rather give him the news in person. I guess we'll be having a margarita tonight, not to celebrate, but to drown my sorrows.

The quiet of the afternoon was interrupted about 4:00 with a phone call from Dr. March. "Annie, I'm glad I caught you! I just got off the phone with that attorney I was telling you about and I wanted to fill you in."

About now, having an attorney didn't seem quite so farfetched as it had earlier. Annie told Dr. March the findings of the peer review committee and Dr. March just said, "It's a good thing you are getting some legal advice. Let me give you his name and number. Call him today and get an appointment set up ASAP. I gave him just an overview of what has happened, but I'm sure he will have questions for you. He's very good, you can trust him."

"Thank you so much, Dr. March, for doing all this for me. I can't tell you how much it means. I'll let you know how things go."

Dr. March didn't have a lot of encouraging words or platitudes like everyone else seemed to have. That actually felt good; it gave Annie a little leeway to feel sorry for herself. You poor thing, such a wonderful person, so wrongly accused and mistreated. A vision of Joan of Arc at the burning stakes made Annie snap back and realize she was going too far.

One quick phone call and she was in touch with the attorney's secretary, a pleasant, wispy voice – an older woman, Annie guessed. The appointment was set to see the attorney, Richard Howe, at ten in the morning. She left a note for Janet explaining the situation. There would be no need of a frantic call to an agency to try to get a replacement nurse. Taking the day off on such short notice would normally have been a major feat involving phone calls, begging and pleading, trading days off, or shifts, making deals with co-workers. "I'll work the late shift for you next Friday, if you can cover for me tomorrow." The late shift was no one's favorite and it carried a special "Friday curse."

Simply put, the curse stated that any nurse who was scheduled to get off duty at 6:00 pm on a Friday evening and had dinner or movie plans would not be leaving until 7:30 at the earliest. But it was easy to get fooled into not believing in the curse. For instance if, at 5:00 pm, there was only one patient left to discharge home and he was pain-free and getting dressed, what could possibly delay his discharge? At 5:30, the Day Surgery phone would ring. It would be the patient's wife, son, or daughter, whoever had been called to come and drive the patient home. There were several scenarios: a flat tire, a misunderstanding, or the caller had just awakened from a late afternoon nap. No matter what, the result was the same. "I'll get there as soon as I can" would be the message. It was at this point that the experienced nurse, having learned to avoid any further frustration and disappointment, would immediately call her spouse and cancel movie plans.

Sometimes a less experienced nurse, not realizing the power of the curse, would foolishly go on believing she could make the movie, just miss the previews of upcoming attractions. She would even, as the minutes ticked on, put the patient in a wheelchair and go to the first floor drive through. Naively, she planned to whisk the patient into the car as soon as his ride pulled up, enabling her to maybe leave work by 6:15.

On course this plan was doomed to fail. As a result of the Friday curse, the patient's ride: A. "got all turned around and lost" or B. went to an entirely different day surgery unit to pick up the patient. If the ride did happen to show up on time, a second scenario unfolded. There were several variations, but the end result was the same. The patient, who had been sitting perkily in the wheelchair, suddenly did one or more of the following: A. began vomiting, B. got pale and fainted, or C. the bandage on his operative site inexplicably fell off or became saturated with blood.

However, when one's only duty was to the policy and procedure book, none of these things could happen. "I guess there are some good things about not being in patient care," Annie mused, "a tiny silver lining in an otherwise black, cloud-filled day."

Annie and Ben pulled into the driveway almost together. Bear, the dog, couldn't decide who to lick first so she just ran around them in circles, making it impossible to walk. After Annie's five minute shower, she was ready to hit the Mexican restaurant with Ben. Over crispy chips and salsa, she shared with Ben the depressing news of what she was facing. Although Ben tried to be understanding, he kept inserting logic into the whole situation which was irritating. It did make sense that this would all be resolved and Annie would be back at work, but things just didn't seem to be happening that way. As they were finishing the fajita taco salad (Annie's with chicken so it was low fat – who was she kidding after two bowls of chips?), Ben stared at her.

"What is that?"

"What is what, Ben?"

"Where did you get that necklace? Is it new?"

Annie reached up and touched the heart.

"Oh, no, how could I forget? Ben, this is Mrs. Lindsey's necklace."

"What are you doing wearing her necklace?

"No, Ben, how could I forget? She gave it to me to keep for her. She is in the hospital. She had surgery this afternoon. I was supposed to check on her cat and water her flowers. She was counting on me . . ."

She put her head down in her hands. Annie had let her sweet neighbor down for the second time today.

When they got home, she went straight next door. There she sat and petted Miss Prissy for a half-hour, to make up for her sins. Miss Prissy didn't realize she had been forgotten and purred loudly, her little diesel motor running contentedly as she snuggled in Annie's lap, which made Annie feel more guilty.

■ ■ ■

Before going to bed, Annie called the hospital to check on Mrs. Lindsey. After doing some tracking she found out that patient Lindsey was in PCU (room 404). When she finally connected to the room, the phone rang repeatedly but no answer.

She transferred back to the nurse's station and tried in vain to get an update.

"I'm sorry, due to the privacy laws I can only confirm we have a patient Lindsey. You are not on the list of people I can give information to."

"You mean she has someone listed? She doesn't have any family."

"I'm really sorry; I cannot give any information, that's just the law."

"I called the room and there's no answer."

"Well, I guess you'll have to come and visit. If you get your name on the list of people that information can be released to, then we won't have this problem. It is a Federal law, I could get into trouble if I broke the rules. It's policy."

Annie decided to go by the hospital after the lawyer's appointment in the morning. *I'm sure she's alright* – Annie's denial mode was functioning extremely well. Blissfully ignorant, she drifted off to sleep.

8

MEMORANDUM

STATUS: C ONFIDENTIAL
TO: MR. EVANS, CEO
FROM: RISK MANAGEMENT
AFTER REVIEW WITH THE HOSPITAL ATTORNEY, WE BELIEVE THAT THE NURSE INVOLVED IN THE RECENT CODE 13 DID NOT ADHERE TO HOSPITAL POLICY. SHE WAS ON THE HOSPITAL PROPERTY AT THE TIME OF INCIDENT. EMPLOYEE SHOULD BE REPORTED TO LICENSING AUTHORITY. SUBSEQUENT DISCIPLINE SHOULD LEGALLY ABSOLVE HOSPITAL OF LIABILITY.

D riving to the lawyer's office, Annie clutched the directions crumpled tightly around the steering wheel. Her palms were sweaty and the ink had smeared. She always had trouble with directions and Ben had started the morning off wrong, as far as she was concerned.

"You better leave an hour early, Annie. The morning traffic is so unpredictable and you always get lost."

"Gee, thanks a lot," Annie snapped back with irritation. Inwardly she knew that Ben was just stating a well-documented fact.

On top of that, it drove her crazy when Ben, who knew her directional handicap, would say, "go east three miles," knowing that Annie had utterly no concept of east/west or north/south.

"Ben, tell me left or right, not east or west, you know I can't figure that out."

"Whoops, sorry, Hon. I grew up a country boy, it's in my DNA I guess."

"Well my DNA has that part missing, as you well know by now, okay?"

Thus the sweaty palms as she struggled to follow the directions. Turning left on Milam, she suddenly realized with a mix of complete surprise and relief she had actually arrived at the correct destination. Due to Ben's major pre-planning timing, she was thirty minutes early.

The office was imposing, mostly glass and steel, landscaped with a few desert-like plants that were probably plastic – very expensive plastic. The woman's voice that Annie had decided was elderly and frail in fact belonged to an attractive thirty-something with laryngitis. She whispered a good morning and introduced herself as Ms. Kelsey. Her makeup was perfect and understated. As she leaned forward in greeting, a strand of her hair, blond and smooth, gently fell sexily over one eye. Immediately, Annie's frumpy factor zoomed to ten and she wished she had used more hair mousse and worn her skinny suit.

"Coffee, Mrs. Brown?"

"That would be great, thanks. I know I am a few minutes early. I wasn't sure how bad traffic would be." *Also, my husband used fear and intimidation tactics which made me doubt I would ever arrive here.*

"Actually, Mr. Howe is here early so you will be able to see him shortly."

After only a couple of sips of her coffee the phone buzzed. Ms. Kelsey answered and spoke briefly.

"You can see Mr. Howe now." Just then, the door behind Ms. Kelsey's alcove opened and a man, presumably Mr. Howe, stepped out.

"Mrs. Brown, Richard Howe." A tall man with silver white hair reminiscent of TV's Matlock (but this Matlock was in an expensive suit, not a rumpled, seersucker one) greeted Annie. His voice was smooth but with an edge, and she could picture the booming tones of 'Objection, your honor' causing the courtroom proceedings to halt immediately. He was a little scary. As he extended his hand to her, she saw the crooked deformity of rheumatoid arthritis in his fingers. This small flaw in his otherwise powerful persona made him suddenly softer.

"Please come in." He gestured to a leather chair across from his steel desk. The chair appeared to be the only comfortable piece of furniture in the room. Everything was brushed metal or had points and angles. Was he like his furniture? A nice cushioned chair in velvet or chenille and maybe some throw pillows on the unwelcoming couch would have softened the place up considerably. He interrupted her mental redecorating with little warning.

"Melinda told me all about you. She thinks very highly of you and is concerned about your being treated fairly."

Dr. March's first name must be Melinda, Annie deduced.

"Mrs. Brown, please just tell me in your own words what happened," Mr. Howe sat with a yellow note pad in hand, focused and nodding his head slightly in encouragement.

"I really think this all goes back to the blanket warmer, when I had it moved back and Nita got so mad at me, I thought she was going to hit me or something. Then there was Mr. Allen. I didn't make him change clothes because . . ."

At this point, Mr. Howe stopped things, a look of puzzlement on his face.

"I'm a little confused. The incident I am interested in is you finding a body in the parking lot. What exactly does a blanket warmer have to do with that?"

Annie stopped and realized she had gone into major rambling mode. "Mr. Howe, I'm sorry. When I get nervous I tend to ramble. I have just been remembering Nita and how much she hates me and I guess it was just the first thing to come to mind. I'll do better now."

Mr. Howe looked a little skeptical, but Annie began carefully recounting the parking lot incident in a coherent fashion. He made one or two notations, but listened without further comment.

"Annie – may I call you Annie? One question. I'm not sure I understand why you were concerned that this person could have been a murder victim."

"I know it sounds silly now, as I tell you, but at the time I was quickly trying to figure out what had happened. It was so dark because of the fog. I think maybe I had been thinking of a murderer that appeared out of nowhere in a fog in a mystery I had just been reading. I read a lot of murder mysteries. I find them relaxing – trying to figure out the identity of the murderer." It was here Annie heard herself rambling again and felt she was making a bad impression on Mr. Howe, as some eccentric who lived out her life through fiction. "Mr. Howe, I'm sorry I got off topic there again a little, I am actually a very stable person." *Hmmm, I don't think stable people usually have to announce how stable they are.* "Anyway, the main thing is, I wouldn't have done anything differently because no matter what the cause, Mr. Olmos had been dead a while —too long to have been resuscitated."

"Well, in my opinion, Annie . . ." here Annie held her breath, in fear of how the sentence would be ended.

" . . . you are completely legally covered by the good Samaritan law. You stopped to render aid, and did so using your best judgment. Even if you caused harm, which you didn't, you still are not liable. Why this is going for review to the State Board of Nursing is somewhat a mystery to me. However, I will be more than happy to represent you at the hearing. It should be brief and routine, unless you have left out some major piece of incriminating information."

At this, Mr. Howe looked at Annie, raising his silver brows in an unspoken question.

"No, no. That is the whole truth, and nothing but the truth, so help me God," Annie blurted out in a louder voice than she intended.

Mr. Howe gave a little chuckle. "I'm your lawyer, Annie. You don't have to take an oath to me. Just go home and try to relax. Don't read any more murder mysteries for a while. I'll contact the board and find out the date of the hearing and be in touch with you."

They parted with a handshake and Annie felt more confident than she had in a good while.

Mrs. Lindsey was in the forefront of her mind as she drove away from her meeting. When she got to the hospital, she went straight to Room 404 in PCU. Knocking gently on the door, and hearing no response, she pushed it open a crack. Seeing the partial outline of a patient in the bed, she softly called out, "Mrs. Lindsey, it's me, Annie."

As she entered the room, the figure in bed roused and turned to face her. She found herself looking at a large black man, in a wrinkled hospital gown. They both stared at each other in a mutual moment of confusion.

"Young lady, I'm Mr. Lindsey. There is no Mrs. Lindsey any longer, she's been gone seven years now."

"Oh, I'm so sorry. I saw the last name and . . . obviously, I made a mistake. I'm so sorry I disturbed you."

"Mistakes happen, don't worry about it. Could you do me a little favor while you're here?"

"Sure, what do you need?"

"My water pitcher needs ice. I'm supposed to be drinking a lot, and I got to have my water cold."

Annie took the pitcher and returned with an ice-filled one shortly. She poured Mr. Lindsey a glass, he thanked her, and she left on her search for the elusive Mrs. Lindsey.

Deciding the easiest way was to check the patient census on the computer, she headed for Janet's office. After going through the list twice, Annie was stumped. Where was Mrs. Lindsey? Could she have been transferred to another hospital or maybe already discharged and was at home petting Miss Prissy?

Just then Janet came in. Annie explained her dilemma to Janet who, being in management, had access to more computer information than Annie.

After just a few moments Janet looked up from the screen and as her eyes met Annie's, she spoke in a solemn voice, "Annie, she expired yesterday afternoon."

After a stunned silence, Annie asked, "What could have happened, Janet? Can you find out any more for me? She was my neighbor and my friend. She was counting on me, she even asked me if she was doing the right thing – having the bronchoscopy – and I told her yes. Thanks to me and my advice, she's dead now. Why, why didn't I do something? And all she ever did was be nice to me and bring me roses from her garden." Annie collapsed in the chair as if she were a puppet whose strings had been suddenly cut.

"I'll find out what happened and I'll let you know. I promise. That's all I can do, Annie, I'm really sorry about this."

Annie decided she had had about all of Trenton James General Hospital she could take for now. When she got home, she went straight to Mrs. Lindsey's to spend some time with Miss Prissy, who was cheerfully unaware that her favorite person would never be coming home to her. She purred happily as Annie stroked her and cried. There had to be an explanation for Mrs. Lindsey's death and Annie determined then to find it, even if it meant breaking the rules. There were some things that were more important than stupid idiotic hospital rules and if this wasn't one of them, she didn't know what was. Guilt, Annie's ever-present companion, wasted no time in trying to convince Annie that Mrs. Lindsey's death was her fault and hers alone. She kept remembering Mrs. Lindsey, with her trusting eyes, asking Annie if she was making the right decision as she signed her operative consent. That piece of paper ended up being her death warrant.

The next afternoon when Annie came home and went for her daily visit with Miss Prissy, she unlocked the door and called softly, "Miss Prissy, it's me," as she walked to the counter with Mrs. Lindsey's mail, glancing through it out of habit. Suddenly she was face to face with a man standing on the other side of the counter. In silence, each sized the other up, as to intent and danger.

The man spoke first, "I'm Elizabeth's cousin, David Windsor. Good afternoon. And you would be . . .?"

"Oh, I'm Annie Brown, the next door neighbor. I thought Mrs. Lindsey didn't have any family. At least, that's what she told me." Annie's breathing was starting to slow down to normal again as her adrenaline levels fell.

He was round and soft-looking, with a silver moustache and matching beard. All together, he had a Santa Clause quality and a proper British accent which added substantially to his charm.

"Well, good afternoon, Annie. Elizabeth didn't have any family in the states and I'm the only one left. Elizabeth and I kept in touch by post. I am not able to travel much, but I came as soon as I got word. Not sure quite where to begin and all, you know."

He looked around surveying the room packed with furniture and knick-knacks in perfusion on every available bit of space. The death, the house and all it's contents must be very overwhelming to this old gentleman.

"Yes, it is a lot. Could I be of any help? Maybe box things up for you, or . . . Mrs. Lindsey loved collecting things didn't she? She was such a sweet lady. I've been taking care of the cat and mail and I wondered what was going to happen to all her things."

"She was a dear, dear lady. She had lost much in her life, but she never lost her faith in God or in people. A remarkable feat, don't you think?"

They stood together in a moment of silence for Mrs. Lindsey. Miss Prissy interrupted as she ran up to Annie with a welcoming meow. Annie picked her up and cuddled her. Mr. Windsor seemed unaware of the cat's presence.

"Yes, Annie, I could use some boxes if you know where some are."

Annie quickly agreed and turned to leave when she absentmindedly fingered the little heart pendant around her neck.

"Mrs. Lindsey gave me this to keep for her when she went to surgery. That's the last time I saw her." She began to undo the clasp but Mr. Windsor stopped her.

"No, Annie, you keep that. I'm sure that's what Elizabeth would want. Besides, it looks better on you than it would on me, don't you think?"

A quick movement of the mustache made Annie realize there was a faint smile underneath it.

"Well, thank you Mr. Windsor. I will treasure it. Okay, then, I'm off to find some boxes. I'll be back in a little while." After putting a scoop of cat food in the empty dish by the door, she left on her mission.

The liquor store up the street seemed to have a never-ending supply of boxes, always left in jumble just beside the entrance. This gave testimony to the daily intake of alcohol in the neighborhood, which had to be sizable by sheer daily volume of cardboard. But it did come in handy when one wanted packing boxes. After loading up, Annie decided Mr. Windsor could probably use a hamburger. As the girl at the counter said, "Welcome to What-a-burger, have it your way," Annie realized she had no idea what Mr. Windsor's hamburger preferences were. For that matter, he may have never had a hamburger before. So she ordered it her way – extra lettuce, tomato, mustard only – and just hoped for the best. He seemed grateful but unsure when she handed him the sack. A look at Mr. Windsor's roundness told Annie he would soon figure out the hamburger. As she left she promised him she would return tomorrow after work and help pack.

After a few days, they developed a routine. Annie reported for work right after she came home from the hospital. The time varied, but Mr. Windsor never seemed aware. He always looked up with a "there you are, my girl" and gave her an assignment. He was shipping everything back to England and the house was being listed with a real estate agent that Annie knew. One day Annie asked him about Miss Prissy's future. He raised his eyebrows and said, "Oh, my, I hadn't thought of the cat." Looking at Annie in a steady way, he never spoke a word.

"Are you thinking I'm going to take her? I'm not sure. I have a dog already and I don't know if Ben would be alright with that. I need to ask him . . ."

At this point, Annie's guilt woke up from a short nap and reminded Annie, If it weren't for you, Mrs. Lindsey would still be here to take care of Miss Prissy. Have you forgotten about that?

And with that, Annie capitulated quietly. "Let me just check with Ben to be sure, Mr. Windsor, but I bet it will be fine."

"Thank you so much, my dear. That will just be one less chore for me to deal with. The little creature seems to be attached to you anyway, you know." And it was true. Miss Prissy's joy at seeing Annie every day was hard to deny.

■ ■ ■

"For crying out loud, Annie, what were you thinking? We don't need or want a cat, we never have."

Oh, good, at least he's going to be reasonable.

"Ben, she's really a sweet little cat. I brought her over for a visit yesterday and Bear and she got along just fine. If we don't take her I'm scared she'll go to the pound. You know people don't adopt adult cats, only kittens. She won't make it. Plus, Mrs. Lindsey already died. I just can't live with Miss Prissy's blood on my hands, Ben, I just can't do it." Annie put her head down in her hands and wondered how many more innocents would suffer because of her.

Ben was suddenly moved with compassion, or at least able to accept defeat when it was obviously inevitable. "Okay, Hon, we can take the cat. But we'll have to probably spend a hundred dollars to get her shots and all, and then she'll need surgery and then it will be more money. So I'm doing this for you but under protest, understand?"

Annie got up and went to Ben and gave him a big hug. "Thanks honey, it'll be okay, I'm sure. You know Mrs. Lindsey took good care of Miss Prissy. I'm sure her shots are all up to date, but I'll see if I can find any papers on her. This will help out Mr. Windsor so much, too. He's pretty exhausted. I was thinking of asking him over for supper tomorrow. It may be his last day here."

"What, we have to take the cat and now the old man too? Come on, Annie, you are asking a lot all at once."

"I thought I would make fajitas and serve a real Tex-Mex dinner. How would that be? I could get some of those tortillas from the Tamale Shack and make some of my special guacamole. You will like him, Ben. He has this great accent; it's like talking to a Duke or something." Annie was so relieved to have rescued Miss Prissy she felt almost giddy. And the thought of entertaining Mr. Windsor for an authentic local meal sounded like a little happy adventure. She knew Ben would like him once he met him.

"Just what I always wanted, to talk to a Duke. Oh well, since I get your fajitas and guacamole out of it I guess I can suffer through an evening. One thing, though, can we change that cat's name? I'm not going to go around calling out 'Miss Prissy', that's asking just one thing too much."

"Do you have any suggestions? I mean, it needs to sound like her old name; maybe Sissy or Missy? You can't name her 'Killer' or some crazy macho name."

"Let me think about it. I'll come up with something. But if I'm agreeing to take the cat, I get to name her. Period."

Annie could sense inevitable defeat as well, and just had to hope for the best. So the next evening, after a wonderful meal with fajitas (beef AND chicken) plus all the trimmings for Mr. Windsor to enjoy, Cat came to live with them.

■ ■ ■

The next few weeks fell into a pattern. Annie worked 8:00 to 4:30 pm, Monday through Friday, always off duty on time.

I wonder what poor sap would be reviewing the policy and procedure book if I wasn't on suspension. Whoever it is owes me big time, for sure.

Going to the lounge for lunch was easier now. Her leper-like feelings seemed to be fading slowly. Christine and Teresa continued to be her staunchest friends, but even Lee surprised her with a breakfast taco one morning.

Annie's work routine was boring but safe. That all changed when she stepped off the elevator early one Monday morning on her way to the office and her old friend, the policy and procedure book. She stood face-to-face with two of Mrs. Olmos' daughters.

"Annie, we were going to find you. Please come see Mama. She's in room 214. She have a fever and she asked about you."

"Oh, I'm so sorry she's not feeling well. I'll come see her this morning, tell her so." Annie knew patient care was forbidden, but just a quick visit to say hello wasn't really patient care. *I can't refuse to go. I'll pop by for five minutes; no one even has to know. It's not fair to hurt Mrs. Olmos' feelings just because I'm in trouble.* That was Annie's line of thinking. Simple and uncomplicated, it also was very flawed reasoning, given her present legal situation.

After hitting the policy and procedure book for a couple of hours, she told Janet she was taking a short break and walked out of the office and straight to room 214. A quick, soft knock and she was in.

Mrs. Olmos lay in bed, surrounded by family. Two small boys played with toy cars on the windowsill, making "car noises." A soft flutter of Spanish conversation floated through the room. Mrs. Olmos' three daughters and several other family members were scattered about. Every available chair was taken and there was a blanket on the floor in a corner where three little girls played quietly together. On top of the other sounds the television was on, the host of a game show describing a trip to Hawaii as excited contestants squealed.

Mrs. Olmos was a short lady, and she had slid down in the bed pretty badly. Her feet were almost touching the metal footboard and her neck was bent at an uncomfortable looking angle.

"Mrs. Olmos. Let's get you scooted up in bed, you're all scrunched up."

"Annie, you always know what to do." Mrs. Olmos looked up with a smile.

You are one of the only people on the planet who think that.

Annie gently lowered the head of the bed and expertly repositioned Mrs. Olmos. Then she slowly elevated her head again and fluffed the pillows.

"Is that high enough, or do you want to be higher?"

"It's perfect, Annie, thank you. I miss you . . . you okay?"

"Yes, Mrs. O. I have been assigned a different job for a while, that's all. I'm sorry you are back in the hospital."

"I have a fever and my back hurts. Maybe I go home tomorrow, the doctor tell me. My heart hurts a lot, though."

"Your heart, what do you mean?"

"Oh, my heart so sad without mi esposo. I think so many times of him. I think how he died and no one help him. The nurse who found him just left him there."

"Mrs. Olmos, how do you know that?" A small doubt flitted across Annie's brain – *maybe I shouldn't be here, maybe I should leave now.* She chose to ignore it.

"I hear some of the nurses talking . . ." She paused and looked vacantly at the TV. Then, remembering herself, she continued, "my brother, he talked to a lawyer. The lawyer told him it's wrong to leave a person like that nurse did."

At this point, Annie should have quietly excused herself. If Mr. Howe were here right now, he would arch his silver brows and warn, "Mrs. Brown, for your own good, you need to leave immediately. Make no further statements without me present, do you understand?"

But fortunately, or unfortunately, depending on one's perspective, Mr. Howe was safely ensconced in his steel and glass office, far away. Annie remembered the verse about the truth setting us free. She looked into Mrs. Olmos' brown eyes that were liquid with tears.

"Mrs. Olmos, I was the one who found Mr. Olmos in the parking lot that morning. I didn't leave him."

Mrs. Olmos looked at Annie in blank surprise. "Annie, you?"

"Yes, me. I would never just walk away from a person in trouble. He had already passed a good while before I found him. His heart was gone already. I got help, but I didn't leave him, I promise."

Mrs. Olmos didn't speak – the two little boys' car noise stopped, the soft flutter of Spanish conversation in the room was gone. The only noise as Annie ended her confession was the wild cheering and applause on the TV game show as the winner of the trip to Hawaii was announced.

Annie looked only at Mrs. Olmos. Mrs. Olmos looked only at Annie. Both had tears but through hers, Annie saw a faint smile appear on Mrs. Olmos' face.

"Oh, Annie, I am so happy you were with mi esposo and you no leave him. Gracias a Dios." She took Annie's hand and planted it on her face in a caress.

Annie was softly sobbing. The awful weight of that secret was lifted. The one person who mattered most understood. Finally she took several deep breaths and said, "Thank you for understanding and believing me. I wasn't going to tell you but you have a right to know the truth. I probably won't get to come back to see you for a while but just know that I care. Okay?"

"Why you no can come back, Annie? I no understand."

"I really don't understand either, Mrs. Olmos. I'll get in touch with you or your daughters when I can. You take care, do what the doctor says, and get strong again. Your family all need you. A lot of patients I see are all alone, but you have "muchas personas" who love you." The overflowing room of people was evidence of that truth. Annie reached over and embraced this dear lady. As she started to leave the room, one by one, the three daughters came up and in turn each gave Annie a wordless hug. She walked out with no regrets, no matter what Mr. Howe's advice would have been.

Annie had assumed that her visit would go undetected but she had not planned on crying and getting her trademark swollen, red eyelids with nose to match. When she walked back into the office, Janet looked up and immediately a shocked expression came over her face.

"Annie, what is wrong? What happened, are you alright?"

"Yeah, I'm more than alright. Mrs. Olmos understands; she understands. I just went over to say hello to her, her daughters were looking for me . . ."

Janet interrupted, "you went to see her? After all that has happened, what could you have been thinking? Those people are ready to sue and your name is in the middle of it all."

"I know, I know. It was just supposed to be a quick hello. She is one of my favorite patients, and I'm always the one she wants to start her IV when she comes in. One thing just led to another, and she was so upset that the nurse that found her husband walked away and left him, I just had to tell her it wasn't true. She is so thankful that I was the one that found him and that I didn't leave him. We hugged and cried together. I know everything is going to work out okay."

Janet, still surprised at Annie's lack of judgment, was irritated and not nearly so optimistic. "You don't know that everything is going to be okay. People under emotional stress are very unpredictable. After a lawyer talks to her, she might change her mind completely. You need to tell your lawyer what you did, and don't go visit her ANYMORE, unless it is approved by him."

"Sure, Janet, I'll do what you say. But in my heart, I know she deserved to know the truth."

"All that "in your heart" stuff may sound right and noble, but you have no idea what a lawyer can do with what you may have said innocently. I'm serious, Annie."

"Janet, don't worry. I won't sneak over there anymore." She could see how wrong it may have looked. But she, not Janet, was the one who had looked into Mrs. Olmos' eyes. No one could convince her of the folly of what she had done.

She hadn't reckoned on Mr. Howe, however. He was somewhere between furious and enraged when she called him that afternoon.

"If you want me to continue to represent you, Mrs. Brown, you have to follow my instructions without question. I didn't instruct you not to see this lady because I thought you had better sense than that. I see I was incredibly wrong."

Annie had to grovel, make repeated promises of obedience, and give Mr. Howe dictator-like power over her whole life before he relented. He was still muttering comments questioning the level of her intelligence as the phone call came to an end. Annie was reduced to simply mumbling "I'm sorry" whenever there was a lull in his muttering.

I don't think I'll mention the visit to Ben for now. She wasn't ready to take on anybody else for the present.

As she was leaving work, Janet stopped by her desk. "Just so you don't think I've forgotten, I have been trying to find out about the death of your friend. I just don't have any information yet. But I am still working on it and I'll tell you when I know. Don't go doing any snooping on your own, though."

Annie said of course she wouldn't do anything like that. In light of her secret visit with Mrs. Olmos, her words lacked credibility with Janet, understandably.

The next day, as she sat in the office staring at the policy and procedure book, the phone's ringing was a timely interruption. Annie was just moments from going to sleep sitting straight up. When she first heard Mr. Howe's voice, she inwardly cringed and wanted to cover her ears but resisted.

"Mrs. Brown, good morning. Haven't made any more surprise visits, have you?"

"No sir, I gave you my word. I won't break it."

"Just how you could have ever decided that was the right thing to do, to see that lady, is just . . ." Mr. Howe paused, actually seeming to be at a loss for words – possibly a first, Annie thought.

"Well, we won't go down that road again. Let me tell you why I called. I talked to the State Board and they have given us a date for the hearing. I wanted to let you know so you can make the necessary arrangements. It is two weeks from today – Tuesday, August the second. It just so happens I will already be in Austin for another commitment so I will meet you there on the morning of the hearing, say at 10:00 am in the lobby. Do you have the address?"

"No, but I'm sure I can find it."

"Call my office, Ms. Kelsey has it and can give you the directions. It is just a few blocks north of . . ."

Annie interrupted Mr. Howe gently. "Mr. Howe, it's okay, I don't want to tie up your time any longer. I will get there on time, don't worry." She didn't want to listen to any more directions that she couldn't comprehend, either.

They hung up on a more cordial note than their earlier conversation.

When Janet heard of the upcoming hearing she turned to Annie, "I am going to drive you up. Don't even think anymore about it. I will go in to the questioning with you, too, if they will let me. Soon we will get this over and done with."

"Thank you so much. I would really appreciate you driving and your company. I'll pay for the gas and take you to lunch."

"That's not necessary, Annie, I want to go with you. The drive to Austin is a pretty one, I like to go out 290 north and . . ." *Oh, no, more directions again.*

Ben, of course, offered to go and drive her too. But Annie wanted to have Ben to come home to. Plus, he would have had to take a paid vacation day off. She would rather save those days for an actual vacation to Padre Island when this was all over. Also, when Ben got worried about her he tended to get in his parental mode and give a lot of directions, and that always got on her nerves. "Whatever you do, don't say . . ." that thought would be planted in Annie's mind and she was scared she would be so nervous she would do the very thing Ben had warned against. In the end, he relented and agreed that Janet could take her.

"Does she need directions? Because I can tell her how I like to go. It's the best route, I think."

"No, Ben. Thanks a lot, Honey, but Janet drives all over the place and she already told me she has a usual route." *Plus, if I hear one more set of directions I am going to scream.*

■ ■ ■

Tuesday, August the second seemed to advance with breakneck speed. As the alarm sounded at 4:30 on that fateful morning, Annie sat up quickly, as was her habit the moment she heard the alarm. She was completely exhausted. All night long, asleep or awake she had been bombarded by thoughts of questions she could be asked. They ranged from the probable to the bizarre, the worst one being, "Mrs. Brown, please state your full name and your correct weight for the board."

Ben had insisted on taking her out to eat last night. Her stomach was already in knots, though, and she couldn't enjoy the Indian food which was her very favorite. Ben didn't care for Indian food that much, so it was a small act of love for him to take her there unasked. Even the spicy curry dishes had tasted like cardboard to her. She tried to look on the positive side and remember Ben's main advice – tell the truth and let the facts speak. That advice had not produced any results so far, but Mr. Howe was in full agreement.

"Your husband is right, the truth and the facts in this case will exonerate you completely in my opinion. That, and the Good Samaritan Law, which is for cases exactly like this."

Janet honked the horn, a short toot, at 5:00 in the morning out of respect to the neighborhood. A quick kiss to a peacefully snoring Ben and she was out the door. Eerily, there was a fog in the air this morning, a reminder of the foggy morning she found Mr. Olmos. She gave a small shiver and got into the car. Janet still looked sleepy. Being the manager, she never had to work the early shift and Annie realized this was a sacrifice of friendship.

"Janet, sorry you had to get up so early. I know you're not used to being up this time of day."

"No problem, Annie, it's good for me to get up early every now and then – not too often, though," said with a little smile.

They rode in a friendly silence as they headed out of Houston, the only sound being Annie's occasional slurp on her coffee cup. It had a cap with a very small opening, making sipping coffee safe but a little noisy.

Annie had worn her skinny suit. She wanted to look as professional as she could, plus there was that irrational fear that she would have to state her weight. Although she had moussed her hair well, it still had the tendency to collapse and would probably be rumpled looking by the time they got to Austin.

Because of the time, they pulled through a MacDonald's and ordered breakfast, eating as they drove. Maybe it was because of not eating much for dinner last night or maybe it was the "last meal" syndrome that condemned prisoners have; whatever the reason, Annie was really hungry. She got one of her favorites – the MacGriddle egg and sausage sandwich. It was delicious and she did feel better prepared to face what lay ahead. Her suit got a small stain on the collar, but she felt sure she would have time to repair it before the hearing.

As they whizzed past the mile markers, Annie decided this was as good a time as any to ask about something she had been wondering.

"Janet, I keep thinking about Nita. I honestly believe she hates me and I don't understand why. It seems like every time we have an interaction I have done something that irritates her. You mentioned to me once that y'all went to nursing school together. Were you friends?"

"Actually, we were roommates for the first year. I don't know if we were ever close friends but I did see another side of Nita."

"What side did you see? I keep thinking nobody can be that mean all the time."

Janet chewed on her lip as she stared down the highway. After a moment of hesitation she spoke. "I can tell you a little, but I won't reveal any confidences. Understood? And what I tell you doesn't leave this car."

"Sure, Janet, whatever you say."

"Nita is a person who was betrayed by the rules – the rules that say the people that you trust to take care of you won't hurt you. Those people broke the big rule. Do you understand what I'm saying? I'm no psychiatrist but I think that's the reason that rules are so important to Nita. If the rules are kept, she feels safe. When rules are broken, it is very scary to her and she reacts."

Annie silently nodded.

"So, it's not about you, Annie, it's about her. Oh, look, aren't those Indian paintbrushes?" Janet pointed to a mass of orange wildflowers as they drove past.

The Nita conversation was over and Annie, on this day of all days, wanted to feel sorry for herself, not Nita. So, instead of feeling compassion, she just felt irritated at poor Nita for not being a mindless monster after all. As they entered Austin, thoughts of the hearing had become the proverbial elephant in the back seat. Annie knew Janet was thinking about it too, but her chatter had progressed to the ridiculous. She was now talking about maybe going on a tour of the capital building.

"I'm sorry; I can't focus on anything but the hearing. I just want to get it over with. Maybe we can make another trip to Austin and tour the capital some day soon."

"Well, sure, I was just trying to take your mind off things, but you are right, we need to face this hearing first and get that behind us."

Janet, who knew north/south, east/west (she must have been a country girl) easily found the location of the building. Not only could she follow directions, she could parallel park without hesitation. Annie was beginning to feel inadequate. Looking down and remembering the coffee stain on her suit made her feel frumpier.

They found a restroom quickly and were both working on getting the stain out by scrubbing and dabbing. The stain seemed to fade, but a large wet spot remained which was much more noticeable than the stain. On top of that, the mousse hadn't worked. Her hair had a dent in the back where she had rested her head on the drive up. Nothing seemed to remove the dent. It was five minutes till ten, and Annie knew she had to be in the lobby on time for Mr. Howe. She was determined not to do anything else to irritate him.

Sure enough, as they rounded the corner together they almost collided with Mr. Howe. He looked so impressive, silver hair framing his face, almost shining.

"There you are, Annie, good morning. All ready to go?"

"I guess so. Oh, Mr. Howe, this is my manager, Janet Simmons."

They exchanged greetings and Annie sensed that all was forgiven.

He had already found the number of the hearing room where the case was being heard. Just before they went in, he looked at Annie. She could tell he wanted to say something, but was hesitating.

"Mr. Howe, don't worry, I am going to tell the truth and let the facts speak, just like you and Ben said and I'll try not to ramble."

"Oh, yes, I think you'll do fine. It's just you have a large spot on your suit collar."

"There was a little stain and we just removed it and I thought it would have time to dry out. Sorry." *Also, there is a dent in my hair in the back that won't come out.*

"Well, we have to go in now, don't worry about it."

Yes, ha, ha. Now that you've pointed it out, I'm sure I won't think a thing about it.

Together, they opened the door. A blast of arctic air sent Annie into a sudden state of hypothermia; she started shivering within minutes. The temperature of the room must be sixty or below. The Nurse Judge Panel probably held a majority of menopausal judges, she quickly deduced. Besides the temperature, the very air itself was oppressive. And the décor--sparse and hard---those were the two words that first came to mind. Walls glaringly white and bare. Five judges were seated in high-backed chairs at the head of a dark wood T-shaped table. As Annie stood, she became aware of the silence. It infused the room and pressed in on her chest like the force field of an evil alien presence. She glanced up to Mr. Howe and was glad he stood beside her. He seemed to help to balance things out some (her secret powerful force field). Janet had been allowed in, but was asked to sit in the back.

Mr. Howe and Annie approached the sitting judges and Mr. Howe introduced himself as Annie's attorney. The lady in the center nodded her head slightly but did not speak in response. She appeared to be intently studying some papers. Surely the board had all the information and reports sent to them long ago. Annie couldn't imagine what was so interesting.

Finally, the lady spoke.

"Good morning. We have a full day today so let's get started. Mrs. Brown, I am Dr. Nolan and will be the chief questioner."

Annie knew that Dr. Nolan wasn't Dr. Nolan, M.D. She was Dr. Nolan, Ph.D. Most, if not all, of the nurses on the board had started out as RN's but had continued on to get advanced degrees. The more initials behind one's name, usually the further away they were from ever actually touching a patient. Staff nurses, such as Annie, whose main focus was patient care often held these nurses (such as the board members) in unspoken disdain. This disdain was often returned in kind by many advanced degree nurses, towards the lowly staff nurse, so right away Annie felt at a disadvantage.

Dr. Nolan continued, "This hearing should be brief. I will ask you to answer your questions as accurately and honestly as you can. You may begin now and tell us the facts of the incident resulting in your being here today."

Annie took a deep breath, tried to calm her shaky legs, and began. She focused on just the facts and didn't ramble once. At one point when she was talking she heard herself, in an out-of-body way, talking way too fast. But she seemed powerless to slow down. When she finished, she felt she had told the truth completely and let out a sigh.

Dr. Nolan looked down at her notes. "The report seems to indicate you thought Mr. Olmos might be a crime victim. Yet I find no evidence to support that claim. Is there any?"

Annie wanted to talk some more about how foggy it was that morning. Maybe she hadn't emphasized that enough. What she didn't want to do was confess that she read a lot of murder mysteries and her imagination coupled with her shock at discovering a body simply got the best of her. But as these thoughts meandered about in her head at a disgustingly slow pace, she finally said, "No ma'am, no evidence."

"Does anyone else have any questions for Mrs. Brown?"

A mean looking little lady at the end of the row motioned her hand.

"Yes, Dr. McRay, go ahead."

"Mrs. Brown, you were aware of your hospital policy regarding a nurse's responsibility to do CPR until a physician arrives or you are physically unable to continue?"

Annie decided right then this lady was probably related to Nita. But whatever the case, she could do nothing more but answer truthfully.

"Yes ma'am, I knew the policy."

Mr. Howe subtly nudged Annie, so she tried to go on from there.

"Ma'am, I just did not think it right to try to resuscitate someone who's been dead for . . ."

"Mrs. Brown, please just answer the questions asked."

Annie: "Yes Ma'am."

Mr. Howe spoke, "If I may just add as a way of explanation, Annie Brown's personnel record is impeccable and . . ."

"Thank you Mr. Howe. The board has that information already."

Though the room air was icy, Annie felt a bead of sweat on her upper lip and began to feel a little nauseated. This was usually a warning symptom that she was going to faint. She didn't think the board would take kindly to that and hoped things were almost over. Taking a few deep breaths, she held on to Mr. Howe's arm.

Dr. Nolan abruptly asked them all to wait outside while the board deliberated and made a final decision.

The three of them stood in the hallway. Annie felt like she had not said enough or said it at the right time but Mr. Howe seemed unconcerned and said, "There are no facts in dispute. Annie, you did just fine, you didn't ramble at all." He patted her hand in approval.

"I would like to stay and take you ladies to lunch, but unfortunately I am on a tight time schedule today."

"That's okay, Mr. Howe, you were there when I really needed you in that board room. I wasn't nearly as scared as I would have been facing them alone. I knew you were watching out for me and that really helped. Thank you for that." She looked up as she spoke and their eyes met. Mr. Howe smiled the sweetest smile, which changed his countenance from imposing to cuddly.

Just then the door to the hearing room opened and they were motioned back in and Annie and Mr. Howe resumed their positions, standing in front of the board.

Dr. Nolan began, "Mrs. Brown, after review of the facts of the incident, the board has made its decision. While CPR to Mr. Olmos would possibly have been futile, that decision was not yours to make. You were on hospital property and should have followed hospital policy. You are hereby placed on probation for six months. You may return to your previous position with the stipulation that you will have weekly reviews with your immediate supervisor on all your nursing decisions. She will turn in monthly behavior reports to the board's probation committee. At the end of six months, if there are no further judgment lapses, your probation will be lifted."

Annie could not believe what she was hearing. Her heart began beating fast, and she heard her own breathing rate speed up; she was going to cry and she didn't want any witnesses. The injustice of it all was nearly overwhelming and she felt like that giant wave was going to drown her again.

Annie was so lost in trying to keep herself together she was unaware of Mr. Howe at her side. If she was in shock, he was enraged. His voice exploded in the quiet room.

"Has this board decided to throw out the Good Samaritan Law which was written for cases just such as this? Your finding is an outrage! There is no excuse for punishing this very competent nurse who simply used good sense in reasoning that this poor man, Mr. Olmos, was beyond help. When one cannot stop to render aid without . . ."

At this point Dr. Nolan interrupted. "That will do, Mr. Howe. The board does not need a lecture on the Good Samaritan Law or your opinions on the actions Mrs. Brown chose to take, ignoring the hospital policy. No further comments will be entertained. The findings of this board are final, and not open to appeal. You are excused."

Mr. Howe's face was red and his silver hair looked wild. While it was nice of him to defend her, that hadn't done any good, nor had telling the truth. Letting the facts speak was pretty overrated, too, Annie decided with a heavy heart. Mr. Howe put his hand on her shoulder and they walked out together.

The three of them stood in a corner of the hallway once again. Janet looked solemn and kept her eyes towards the floor. Annie was numb. The only thing her poor brain could manage right now was keeping her vital signs and respirations functioning. Mr. Howe, in contrast, was like a man on fire. He clinched and unclenched his fists, ran his hands through his once smooth silver hair, and looked around the hallway repeatedly. Annie thought that if any of the board members came out, he was ready for a fight. As all but one of them were older females, she hoped they stayed put for a while.

"Annie, I don't know what went on in that hearing room, but it doesn't add up. I think the board had made their decision long before we entered the room. Somebody got to them."

"I don't understand what you mean. Who would get to them and why?" As her brain wasn't presently working, she was at a distinct disadvantage.

"The ruling doesn't make any sense. That business about being on hospital property is superseded by the specifics of the Good Samaritan Law and they know that. They may assume that I don't, but they are very much mistaken. 'Quo bono?' Who benefits from this ruling where you, Annie, are blamed and disciplined? Well, suppose there is a possible lawsuit from the family, or the legal department has studied this case and made a recommendation. If the hospital can say, "We placed the offending nurse on disciplinary probation and the State Board will be following her compliance", that may go a long way to exonerate the hospital of blame. Of course, I know of no way to prove any of that, and one thing the board said is true – their findings and rulings are not open to appeal. I can't tell you how sorry I am things have gone this way. I think as long as you comply with the monthly reports, you are okay. I don't think they are interested in getting rid of you; they just need a legal scapegoat. Does that make sense?"

"Mr. Howe, not much of anything makes sense to me right now. But I know you have another appointment today. Janet and I need to get headed back to Houston. Thanks again for trying to help me." Annie didn't want to hear any more complicated explanations. She just wanted to go home to Ben and Bear and Cat and be left alone. They parted in the lobby and Mr. Howe reminded Annie to call him if there were any further problems.

Annie couldn't understand the point of that instruction (what else could possibly happen) but she nodded and she and Janet walked out towards the car. Up to this point, Annie realized, Janet had not said a single word. As they got in the car she was aware of how much she appreciated having Janet and spoke, "Thanks for driving, Janet. I am pretty sure I couldn't manage driving home."

"I'm not sure I can, either," Janet responded softly and Annie saw that she was crying.

"Oh, Janet, don't cry. I'll start and once I start I don't know when I'll ever stop."

"It's just that it is so wrong, the way you have been treated from the very beginning. I am so sorry. I kept thinking things would get straightened out and I have been wrong at every turn." Janet fumbled between the car seats, trying to feel for a much-needed Kleenex. She blew her nose loudly and they both smiled.

"I forgot I was supposed to give you these," Janet was handing Annie a small bundle of papers she had located in the Kleenex search. "Maybe it's better to have them now anyway. Go ahead and open it. I'll drive and you can read everything."

There were several envelopes secured with a rubber band. Annie opened the first. It was a card with a bouquet of flowers on the front. Inside was a note from Teresa, telling Annie what a wonderful nurse she was, how much she had missed her, and how everything was going to be okay. The next card was from Christine, a plain card that was simply signed "from Chris." There were cards from almost every nurse on the Day Surgery staff and one from Dr. March, as well. Each one, in it's own style, communicated concern and care for Annie. It was such a touching gesture, and after the horrendous outcome the words were welcome little hugs.

Annie wanted to say how much she appreciated them, but all she could seem to come up with was, "thanks." She could tell she was holding in her emotions because she was afraid of completely falling apart. Janet seemed to sense that and they drove most of the way back in silence.

Janet drove up into Annie's driveway about 5:00 in the afternoon and as Annie got out she said, "I think you need a few days off. If you want, I'll put in for your two personal days and then you can let me know if you need Friday, too."

"You're right as usual, Janet, Thanks for taking care of that. I'll call you on Thursday and let you know."

Annie, in a quiet haze, walked to the mailbox to grab the mail before Ben got home. One more blow came from none other than the US Mail. As Annie sorted through the small pile, she noticed the quarterly newsletter of the State Board of Nursing. Usually filled with bits of legal advice on nursing issues, it wasn't fun to read but certainly informative. As she always did, she flipped to the last two pages. These contained lists of nurse's names and what disciplinary action had been taken. It varied from the worst (license revoked) to the mildest (warning with stipulation). She always scanned the names to see if she recognized any of her nursing school classmates. Though there was no explanation of why the discipline was being meted out, one could speculate.

Drug abuse, abandoning a patient, maybe killing a patient through a drug error, those kinds of things were what Annie thought of when she read the names.

The next newsletter will have "Brown, Anne" in that list. I wonder how many people are just like me, looking for names and if my old classmates will think I'm on drugs. Really, it was enough to make one want to try drugs. Her sad reverie was interrupted by one who still believed in her – the dog.

Bear greeted Annie with extra licks and nuzzles. That dog was psychic about Annie, for sure. She went in and sat down; the dog planted herself gently on top of Annie's feet, willing her to sit down too. Cat joined them curling up on the couch where she could watch them both. It wasn't long before Annie heard Ben's car pulling up in the driveway. Bear roused up from Annie's feet and went to the back door to greet Ben.

A short whistle announced Ben's arrival. She could hear him talking baby talk to Bear. He came straight to her chair and leaned down and hugged her, kissing her forehead.

"Hon, I was kind of expecting a call. I've been thinking about you all day. What happened at the hearing?" He sat down in the chair next to her, and she felt his love through his undivided attention.

"Ben, it was horrible. It was so degrading. They treated me like a common criminal, whatever that means. I mean, like – is there an uncommon criminal? Are they better than a common one? I am on six month's probation. Every week I have to meet with Janet and she has to turn in a BEHAVIOR REPORT. Like, am I carrying a gun, doing drugs, or what? Like there is something wrong with my behavior! If at the end of the six months I don't have any LAPSES IN JUDGMENT, the probation will be lifted. I never had a lapse in judgment. They said, even though it POSSIBLY would have been futile to do CPR, I still should have done it. I mean, that poor man was dead, had been dead for probably a half hour or more. And the thing of it is, I bet you not one of those board members have been within touching distance of a patient in years, much less ever found a dead person and had to make a quick judgment call. It is so wrong, I just don't think . . ." Here Annie began sobbing loudly and deeply, finally in touch with the hurt and anger of it all.

Ben came and sat on the floor beside her, rubbing her legs softly as she wept, saying nothing. Bear sat on the other side, licking her toes gently, both man and animal trying to give comfort.

Finally, Ben spoke. "Hon, I am so, so, sorry that you had to go through that. You care so much for your patients, and to be accused of misjudging that situation had to hurt. But we will get through this. You know that, don't you?"

"No, I guess I don't. Janet gave me the next two days off. I just need time to process everything. Right now, I don't want anything to do with nursing but I don't want to make any decisions until I have had time to think. I'm just warning you, though, that's how I'm feeling right now. I don't know if that will change or not. One other thing, Ben, I need . . ."

"Whatever you need, Annie, we will do," Ben was quick to emphasize his support.

"What I really need is a Kleenex."

After blowing her nose, and holding a cold washcloth over her eyes for a few minutes, Annie looked in the mirror. She was all red and swollen and that made her start crying again. Ben had left to go pick up some hamburgers at the What-A-Burger. She had forgotten to tell him extra lettuce and tomato on hers. That was her attempt to have a serving of vegetables and mentally justify the hamburger as a healthy meal, remnants of an old membership in Weight Watcher's years ago. Maybe he would remember, but probably not. Ordering fast food was a situation where she and Ben had a major difference of opinion. She didn't mind at all asking for a variation in her order. For Ben, to have to say, "Mustard only please," was almost an unthinkable request, one which could have the most dire consequences, possibly causing the whole restaurant to come to a complete halt (Call the manager, someone has ordered mustard only). So if she didn't accompany him to the restaurant, there was a good likelihood she wouldn't get: mustard only, extra lettuce and tomato. In the scheme of life it was unimportant, but right now she wanted her burger the way she wanted it.

To remedy this, she went into the kitchen and found the lettuce and a tomato. She had just finished washing and slicing things when Ben came back.

"Here's your burger, Hon, just the way you like it – mustard only and extra lettuce and tomato."

Annie starting crying again.

9

MEMORANDUM

STATUS: PRIORITY
SUBJECT: PRE-OP PATIENT PREPARATION
TO: ALL DAY SURGERY PRE-OP NURSES
FROM: NITA STROMEYER, RN NURSING SUPERVISOR
IT HAS COME TO MY ATTENTION THERE HAS BEEN ANOTHER INSTANCE OF HOSPITAL POLICY NOT BEING ADHERED TO WHEN PREPARING A PATIENT FOR THE OR – IE, NOT CHANGED INTO HOSPITAL ATTIRE, LAB WORK NOT COMPLETED. THIS IS UNACCEPTABLE. REFER TO POLICY AND PROCEDURE BOOK, IF NEEDED.

The next two days seemed a haze to Annie, punctuated by long crying spells and short quiet times where she simply sat, trying to figure everything out. Ben gave her space and to his credit, not one word of advice or solutions. She knew he must have chewed on his tongue more than once. Christine, Teresa, and Janet called. Annie didn't answer, but she listened to their messages, which all said they missed her and wanted her back. Janet's message held additional information about Mrs. Lindsey.

"Sorry it's taken me so long, Annie; it's been hard to get information but I finally broke a few rules myself. I found the circulator who was in the OR for that case. She told me that the patient suddenly started hemorrhaging during the scope. She said your friend had a huge tumor in her left bronchus. She doesn't know if a blood vessel ruptured or part of the tumor was dislodged and that started the bleeding. She told me they did everything they could, but they couldn't stop the hemorrhage. Since the patient died on the operating room table, there is a medical staff hearing to be sure there wasn't any incompetence. Those hearings are highly confidential, but if I do ever hear anything else I will tell you. I think we just have to accept what information we have. Maybe it would have happened with any doctor. Annie, we'll probably never know for sure. I hope this helps you a little. Call me when you're ready to come back to work. Everybody misses you."

Poor Mrs. Lindsey, maybe Janet was right though. And no investigation was going to bring her back. It was just one more sad thing right now. She said a prayer asking forgiveness and cuddled Cat a long time.

By Thursday afternoon, Annie felt more certain of a few things. Taking care of patients was what she loved and had always done best. Now her confidence in that ability had been stolen.

I will always be second-guessing myself, tormenting myself every time I have to make a nursing judgment, wondering if the next time Nita will win. I don't think I can practice nursing that way.

She called Janet and told her she would be in on Friday and just needed to know which hours she would be working.

"I'm so glad you are ready to come back to work, Annie. I need someone on the early shift. How about coming in at 6:00 am?"

As she hung up the phone, Ben was just coming in the back door.

"Ben, I need to talk to you. I have come to a decision."

He settled himself in the other brown chair, a slight feeling of trepidation hovering in the background. Sometimes Annie could come up with some unusual ideas. He recalled one that involved raising emus.

"I know things will be tight financially for us for a while and for that I am so sorry, but I just can't go back to nursing, Ben. They stole my belief in myself. It's gone and what's left is pretty sad. I am going in tomorrow and work the day. At the end of my shift, I will give Janet my letter of resignation. I did some internet research and found that the University of Houston has a twelve week paralegal school. I've always been fascinated by the law. I think I would enjoy that, maybe. You know how I like reading mysteries, and courtroom dramas. It is not real expensive and I can get a student loan. What do you think? Is that a good plan?"

Ben looked at Annie. Anything but a resounding 'Yes!' would crush her.

"Honey, that is a great idea. It sounds like you have thought this all through. Don't worry about the money. We will work that out."

"Well, thanks for being on my side. I didn't know if you would think it was some harebrained scheme or not."

The word 'harebrained' actually had briefly crossed Ben's mind, but he would staunchly deny it, even if pressed.

"Are you sure you can work tomorrow? You could always call Janet and tell her, I know she would understand."

"I can't. I don't want to bail out and leave them in a bind. This way they have two weeks to hire and orientate my replacement. I owe them that much."

"Okay, if you're sure, but I can't see how you think you owe them anything. I still think calling Janet would be a good idea."

"Ben, you've been so good these last two days, not giving me advice and trying to solve things. Don't start now, please."

"Okay, Hon. Do it the way you think you need to."

Part of her felt sad and part of her felt powerful as Annie wrote her briefly worded letter of resignation. She simply gave her two weeks notice, no frills or fluffy sounding explanations.

I have to do this to take back my life. Into the envelope, one lick, and her fate was sealed. The deep-inside voice in Annie said something else so softly she couldn't hear it.

When the alarm sounded at 5:00 am the next morning, Annie realized she had slept through the night for the first time since that wretched foggy day in June. As she went through her automated morning routine, she actually felt a lift in her spirit. *It will feel good to be back at work. I have missed Christine and her grouchy self more than I realized.*

Pausing at the time clock she reflected, *I won't be doing this much longer.* Annie stood motionless in front of the bulletin board beside the time clock as she read the brief bulletin trimmed in red ribbon to add to the festive nature of the announcement.

CONGRATULATIONS TO OUR PHYSCIAN OF THE QUARTER, DR. JIM NAGEL. A COME AND GO RECEPTION WILL BE FROM 2PM TO 3PM IN THE HOSPITAL CAFETERIA. PLEASE JOIN US IN HONORING HIM.

Sigh. God, where is the justice?

Christine was already in the dressing room, almost finished changing into scrubs. She looked up and when she saw it was Annie who had entered, a big smile crossed her face. Before Annie could even smile back it was gone, though.

"So you are showing back up and you're not even early? We have been in a real bind without you; it's about time you came back."

"Oh Christine, don't try and cover up, I know you are happy to see me; I know I'm sure happy to see you," Annie wasn't fooled for a minute by Christine's words. She went over and gave her a big hug. "Hello, you old grouch! Thanks for the cards and calls, they really helped me."

Christine mumbled in response, "It was nothing."

Annie started to leave the letter in her locker, but instead quickly slipped it into her scrub jacket along with her scissors. It would be a reminder of her decision and help her get through the day. As they walked out towards pre-op to start the day, it felt like old times again.

She quickly grabbed a chart and went out to call the first name.

"Mrs. Nguyen, please." She hadn't realized that this was the sweet little lady who she had helped transfer to ICU after her post-op complication. But as the tiny lady made her way towards Annie with her daughter beside her, it all came back.

"Why hello there, Mrs. Nguyen. I'm Annie. I remember you, it's good to see you," Annie reached out a hand to greet her.

Not surprisingly Mrs. Nguyen had still not mastered English. She and her daughter, the rather incompetent interpreter, smiled in unison at Annie. Annie was glad that pre-op room one, which held the much-needed language phone, was vacant. The daughter began speaking as they walked together down the hallway.

"Good to see you, Miss Annie. You the one that helped my mother so much. You the one who know what to do. She want to thank you last time, but she not remember your name. Sorry."

"Why, what a nice thing to say. It wasn't all me, we are a team here. We all work together."

"No, that other nurse, she going to send us home, but you know something not right. Thank you so much, my mother want to thank you, too." After a brief aside to her mother began in Vietnamese, Mrs. Nguyen entered the conversation.

"Miss Annie, thank you." It always surprised Annie what things patients figured out sometimes.

"You're welcome, Mrs. Nguyen, but it wasn't only me . . ."

"Dr. Nagel, he say you a good nurse, too." The daughter was insistent on giving Annie credit.

"Dr. Nagel said that about me?" Annie couldn't hide her astonishment.

"Yes, Miss Annie, for sure you."

Mrs. Nguyen reached up and hugged Annie. Knowing Mrs. Nguyen had been on the regimen of TB drugs for a few weeks, Annie felt safe in hugging her back. She would have hugged her back, even if she hadn't felt safe, though.

The preparation of Mrs. Nguyen seemed to go much smoother than last time. Annie really didn't know why. Sometimes things went smooth, sometimes bumpy. As she went out to the desk, she was greeted by Dr. March who was reviewing charts to prepare for the morning cases.

"Oh, Annie, it is so good to have you back. Richard called and told me all about the hearing. He felt so badly for you. He was really upset about the findings. Are you okay?"

"I'm just trying to move on. It hurt, but . . ." Annie didn't want to tell Dr. March her decision and she didn't want to go back to that painful place, she just wanted to get through today.

Dr. March, sensing Annie's discomfort quickly chimed in, "Well, no matter, we are glad you are here. Several of the docs have asked about you. Dr. Alphonse called me just yesterday and asked about you."

Once again, Annie was surprised that her situation even mattered to any of the doctors. "It is nice to know people care, that helps more than anything."

The pre-op desk at 6:30 in the morning was no place for an extended conversation and the phone's ringing focused them on the immediate tasks at hand.

"This is the lab, the specimen on Mr. Cook ya'll sent over didn't have the nurse's initials on it so we discarded it. You need to send another over, if ya'll want a CBC done."

Ah, yes, Annie, welcome back.

As she took the needed information from the lab tech, she had to smile. This was part of her world: missing initials, tracking down lost charts, correcting errors, putting the puzzle together so that everything fit.

Christine tapped her on the shoulder. "Are you free to check in another patient? I can, but I thought you might want to."

"Sure, Christine, where's the chart?"

Christine handed her the chart and she saw the name – Olmos. Mrs. Olmos was on the surgery schedule today, and Annie had been so preoccupied she hadn't noticed.

"I saved room six. I figured you would want the big room, right?"

"Thanks, Christine, I'll go and get her."

As she walked to the waiting room, she quickly spotted the Olmos family clan. The two little boys were there with their toy cars and the whole group moved as one large organism, the daughters rising from their chairs along with Mrs. Olmos as Annie approached.

"Mrs. Olmos, oh, it is so good to see you," Annie said as she reached down and they hugged.

"Annie, I didn't know if you were here or not. You be my nurse, right?"

"Absolutely, I will be your nurse, Mrs. Olmos. Let's go back. We have the big room saved just for you and your family."

Little boys, toy cars and various family members trailed down the hallway in procession with Annie and Mrs. Olmos. Just as before, it seemed that this family filled every nook and cranny of whatever hospital room they occupied.

"Everything is okay with you now, Annie?" Mrs. Olmos looked up questioningly as Annie finished taking her blood pressure.

"Everything is okay, Mrs. Olmos."

This brave little lady fighting cancer, still grieving over the loss of her husband, was worried about her. Annie wondered if she would have that same compassion if their situations were suddenly reversed.

After a lengthy family conference about where Mrs. Olmos' IV should be started, ("Remember, Mama, it hurt last time when you had it in your right hand?") Annie was securing it in place with the last piece of tape when Dr. Grayson walked in.

"Good morning, Mrs. Olmos."

A quick nod to Annie, with eyebrows raised in the unspoken question, "Do you have the patient ready, nurse?"

Mrs. Olmos smiled and spoke a gracious "Good morning, Dr. Grayson, mi familia is all here."

"Yes, I see . . . hello everyone." Dr. Grayson would have to be blind and deaf not be aware of the presence of the Olmos clan. He turned to leave, anxious as always to get on with his busy schedule, but Mrs. Olmos seemed to be in the mood to talk.

"Dr. Grayson, my nurse, Annie, she's back. She's my best nurse."

At this, the doctor was forced to acknowledge Annie. "Yes, I see she's back. Good morning, Mrs. Brown."

Annie smiled a good morning, but Mrs. Olmos was on a roll. With Dr. Grayson a captive audience, she continued, "Annie, she had some trouble, but it not her fault, she's a good person, always good to me and all mi familia."

At this he looked at Annie, mildly surprised, she was sure, that a patient would know about trouble a nurse was having.

"Yes, well, everything is fine now, Mrs. Olmos. It's all okay now," Annie interjected, trying to gracefully bring this topic to an end.

"Well, I no like that you get in trouble. You tried to help mi esposo, just too late."

By this time Dr. Grayson, who had had one hand on the doorway as if holding on would insure his timely exit, had stopped.

"Is that right? I didn't know about that."

Annie closed her eyes. Oh, no, where are you going with this, Mrs. O?

"Mrs. Olmos, good morning." It was the anesthesiologist, Dr. March, innocently interrupting, coming to the rescue once more.

"Oh, hello, Dr. Grayson, I didn't realize you were still with the patient." She had walked into the room with her head down, looking at the lab results on the patient's chart.

Dr. Grayson was then snapped back to his usual busy, fast-moving mode.

"No, that's okay. I will see you back in the OR then." He turned and was gone.

"Good morning, Doctor, how are you?" Mrs. Olmos greeted Dr. March with a smile.

"I'm fine, thank you. I'm Dr. March. I will be your anesthesiologist for your procedure this morning. I'll be putting you to sleep. I just have a few questions."

"Sure, Doctor. I have mi familia with me today." Mrs. Olmos certainly seemed to be in one of her more chatty moods today and she gestured expansively around the room, as if to show Dr. March that all these people belonged to her.

Before Dr. March could even respond, she continued, "and I have my most favorite nurse back." Reaching out, she patted Annie's' hand and looked up with affection.

Annie didn't know if Mrs. Olmos was going to tell the whole story or not, but right now she didn't care much.

"She's one of my most favorite nurses, too, Mrs. Olmos. We are all glad she's back. But we've got to get back to business here. Did you have anything to eat or drink since midnight, Mrs. Olmos?"

■ ■ ■

As soon as Mrs. Olmos was transported back to the OR, the focus quickly shifted: clean the room, wipe down the recliner with antibacterial solution, spot clean any blood drops on the floor that were sometimes evidence of an IV having been started, find out who was next in line, start getting that patient ready, keep things moving. Annie quickly found herself back in that routine without even thinking. It was satisfying to be a part of the team, helping patients through the maze of questions, paper work, instructions, and calming their fears – just a part of what it meant to be a nurse.

Christine and Annie got to break for lunch about noon. The lounge was like a train station, people coming and going, getting paged mid-way through a bite of their sandwich to answer a question, hoping they could finish the sandwich without another page or phone call. Because of such frequent interruptions, nurses became notoriously "fast eaters" and Annie had developed this pattern along with most of her co-workers. It often proved embarrassing when she and Ben went out with friends to dinner. Annie would take the last bite of her steak and look up to see everyone else still placidly munching on their salads.

As she and Christine walked back to pre-op, the door connecting pre-op to the operating room opened with a swish. Rosa, one of the OR nurses, was rapidly approaching them, a woman on a mission. She called out, " Help, please, I need a favor." In her hand was a small plastic specimen container and an orange colored paper Annie recognized as a cytology requisition.

"I need this specimen run to the Pathologist stat. The volunteer must still be at lunch and I can't find anybody to take it. Could one of you help out?"

Annie thought a brisk walk over the walkway and into to hospital to Pathology would do her good after lunch.

"Sure, I can do it. Hand it over."

"Thanks, Annie, the doctor is trying to get clean margins." There was always urgency when trying to get clean margins. Everything was at a standstill in the operating room until the Pathologist examined the specimen that Annie was taking to him and could call and assure the surgeon that all the cancerous cells had been removed and all the edges of the specimen had healthy tissue, or clean margins.

Just as Annie started to walk away, she remembered an important piece of information she was lacking.

"Which OR room are ya'll in?"

"Oh, yes, number three."

Since the Pathologist called directly to the surgeon, it was vital to know which one of the four rooms held this particular patient.

Walking through the hallway, Annie realized she hadn't been back in the hospital since her illegal visit with Mrs. Olmos. That seemed ages ago. As she entered the elevator to go up to Pathology on the third floor, Nita stepped in behind her. She was absorbed in reading something and didn't look up to see Annie until the doors were closing, sealing them in together.

Annie's basic insecurity trumped her angry feelings and she smiled and said, "Good afternoon."

Nita kept her mouth closed, a thin little line drawn on with a fine-line marker, and gave an almost imperceptible nod. The elevator doors opened at the third floor, and they both exited, side by side. Annie couldn't think of another single word to say but the silence was intensely uncomfortable, like an itchy wool sweater on a warm day.

Nita suddenly stopped midway down the hallway. Annie turned briefly and their eyes met.

"I guess you are real proud of yourself, Mrs. Brown."

Yes, being placed on probation for six months is a real feather in my professional nursing cap.

"No, I'm not, Nita; why should I be proud of being on probation?"

"Do not play the innocent with me, Mrs. Brown, I'm talking about the lawsuit being dropped. Just because you play up to this patient and her family and sweet-talk them into dropping the lawsuit doesn't get you off the hook with me. You broke the rules, ignored policy, but I have always seen right through you. You were just damn lucky."

Annie just looked at Nita. The anger and bitterness seemed to drip off of her, like wax from a melting candle. Poor Nita. In a prison of her own making, she just didn't get it. Annie paused, trying to formulate a response. Thoughts of all the care and support she had received from her co-workers, her manager, her special patients, and even from some of the doctors flooded through her mind. Annie smiled. Not a pleasant little smile, an ear-to-ear smile from her toes to her head.

"Yes, Nita, you're right. I really am lucky. I have to get to Pathology stat, have a great day. Oh, yes, one other thing . . . my name is Ann-IE, not Ann-A." She walked away still smiling, while Nita simply stared.

Back at the pre-op desk, Christine was nowhere to be seen. She was in one of the rooms, checking in the last patient on today's surgery schedule. As Annie walked back, Christine called out from where she was working, "Annie, Lee was covering the desk and took a call a minute ago. She told me there was an "add-on" to the schedule today. I think she wrote it down, could you check on it? I don't know if the patient is on his way, or needs to be called, or what."

Annie scanned the schedule sheet. It was covered with various notes and information written by various people during the course of the day. There were patient check-in times, room numbers, notes of cancellations, and sometimes a phone number hastily scribbled by someone using it as the closest available note pad. Written in pencil at the bottom, Annie found that a patient had been added on to have a debridement and possible amputation of two toes on the left leg. Before she could even find the name, the phone was ringing.

"Annie, somebody has got to do something about this patient." It was Maya, the secretary at the check-in desk. Annie could hear the noise of an angry voice in the background. There was something going on in the waiting room.

"I'm on my way," Annie responded as she hung up the phone.

As soon as she entered the waiting room, she heard the shower of obscenities filling the room. As she came closer, she detected the odor of an unwashed body, and she soon recognized the yeller with the foul mouth to be her old friend Mr. Allen, up to his usual tricks, it would seem.

"Mr. Allen, Mr. Allen, what's the matter?"

He turned his attention from poor Maya, who had the "deer in the headlights" look about her. His hair stood on end in places, a wild man in a wheelchair. Annie wasn't sure but she thought that he might be wearing the same stained, plaid shirt she had seen on him before, buttoned up wrong, his shirt collar askew. Still grimy, smelly and angry; the flapping empty pants leg, mute evidence of his old amputation.

"Annie, it's you, girl! This place is a damn unorganized mess. This old biddy here doesn't know her . . ."

"Mr. Allen, I'm sure we can figure this all out, just give me a minute."

At this point Maya interjected, "He says he is having surgery today. He's not on the schedule and no one called me about any add-ons."

Lee had taken the message about Mr. Allen, but must not have called to let Maya know. It did make it seem that nobody knew what was going on, and Mr. Allen was short on patience in the best of circumstances; this wasn't one of them.

"Maya, I'm sorry you didn't get the information."

"Well, yes, that would have been nice." Maya was irritated and Annie couldn't blame her.

Mr. Allen had stopped his tirade momentarily, but had gotten a chance to catch his breath. Hands on the wheelchair, he began to slowly move toward the exit, talking as he went. "Well, this is a damn mess, that's what I have to say about it. Maybe I'll just leave, and go back home since . . ."

"Mr. Allen, let me try and fix things, okay? I'm sure you need to have this surgery today or your doctor wouldn't have scheduled it. I am sorry you thought we weren't ready for you but we are."

"They just want to keep cutting on me. I'm damn sick and tired of all this cuttin'," he stopped, as if he didn't know what to say next. He looked down at the empty pants leg.

"You have had to go through a lot, I know," Annie started speaking softly.

"You don't know, nobody knows, nobody damn knows."

He was right. She could only imagine some of Mr. Allen's suffering. Sometimes, there just weren't any words. She stood by him in a moment of silence and then put her hand gently on his shoulder. She waited. He didn't pull away.

"Annie, this damn foot is killing me. Can you do something about that?"

"Sure, Mr. Allen, I'll take you back and put you on a stretcher and we'll put your leg up on pillows. I'll call Anesthesia and see if I can give you some pain medicine while we are waiting for the doctor. Will that help?"

He didn't answer, just nodded his head.

As they entered pre-op, he added, "And another thing, remember how you don't make me change all my clothes, so it don't hurt so much . . ."

"Yes, I remember, Mr. Allen, we'll do it however you want to try not to make it hurt."

As she carefully eased him up on to the stretcher, his arm around her shoulder for support, he grimaced slightly with the pain and said softly, "Annie, thanks for being so good to an ol' bastard like me."

As Mr. Allen released her from his smelly embrace, she raised up. Suddenly her upward motion stopped, like an elevator stuck between floors. As she had helped Mr. Allen to the stretcher, her scrub jacket had gotten caught. He was lying on part of it. As she gently tugged and eased it out, she heard a small crumpling sound. Retrieving the last corner of her jacket, she was able to stand upright and as she did, the letter fell from her pocket. It was badly bent and had a small brownish stain, origin unknown, on the front. As she held it in her hands, she knew. She leaned over and tapped the foot pedal to open the trashcan beside Mr. Allen's stretcher. Its' small metal mouth opened, swallowed the stained letter, and closed with a small clank.

"I bet you would like a warm blanket, Mr. Allen."

"Yeah, Annie, that sounds good."

Epilogue

The letter from England was waiting for Annie when she got home:

Dear Annie,

My dear girl, I have been so remiss not to have properly thanked you for all your help and kindness to me when I was in the States. It is only after coming home and sorting through things, I realized I had been so distracted by losing Elizabeth and all that entailed from that, I didn't appreciate my next-door neighbor angel---you. Thank you for that wonderful hamburger you brought me the first day. Thank you also for the lovely authentic Texas meal you prepared on my final night. And last but not least, thank you for taking on the care of Elizabeth's cat. I know that would have meant so very much to her.

As a small token of my thanks, please accept this check. I know this is what Elizabeth would have wanted. Maybe you and Ben can go on holiday together sometimes soon.

All my best to you both!

Sincerely,
David Windsor

And enclosed was a check to Annie Brown for $5000.00

Kathleen Bateman has been an RN for over 35 years. This is her first novel.

She lives in the Houston area with her husband and psychic black dog. She is currently working on the next Annie Brown novel.

www.ingramcontent.com/pod-product-compliance
Lightning Source LLC
Chambersburg PA
CBHW051512170626
46811CB00002B/791